CIRCLE

OF
GOLD

CIRCLE

OF

GOLD

CANDY
DAWSON
BOYD

SCHOLASTIC
HARDCOVER

Scholastic Inc.
New York

No part of this publication may be reproduced in whole or in part, or stored in a retrieval system, or transmitted in any form or by any means, electronic, mechanical, photocopying, recording, or otherwise, with___ written permission of the publisher. For information ___ write to Scholastic Inc., 555 Broadway, N ___

Circle of gold / Candy Daw___
          p.   cm.
    Summary: Mattie is determined ___ her mother a beautiful gold pin for Mother's Day, even though ___ saved enough money and has just lost her job.

          ___N 0-590-49 ___

[1. Mother's Day — Fiction. 2. Gifts — Fiction. 3. Money — Fiction.]
I. Title.
PZ7.B69157C1   1994
[Fic] — dc20

                                                            93-19020
                                                                 CIP
                                                                  AC

12 11 10 9 8 7 6 5 4 3 2 1   2   4 5 6 7 8/9

                          Printed in the U.S.A.   37

For the children

CIRCLE

OF

GOLD

ONE

Mattie curled herself into the warm center of the bed and listened for the early morning sounds of her mother and twin brother — kitchen sounds and bathroom sounds. But the apartment was silent. On the count of three, she told herself, she would get up.

One . . . one and a half . . . two . . . two and a half . . . three. . . . Mattie threw back the covers and jumped out of bed. When her feet touched the cold, smooth wooden floor she caught her breath and raced out of the bedroom.

A quick check of the apartment told her that Mama wasn't there. Mattie stopped to pick up the newspapers scattered on the living-room rug. Since Daddy had died, Mama had lost all interest in keeping the place neat.

Walking down the narrow hallway again, Mattie

paused by her mother's room. The empty bed with its wrinkled white sheets and tossed pillows looked like a stormy sea.

Continuing down the hall, Mattie peeked into her brother's room. She could just see the top of Matt's curly head poking above the covers. His drawing pad was on the bed and the easel he used for his paintings stood against the window, draped with a sheet. The jars of water he used to wash his paintbrushes were lined up like colorful sentries along the windowsill.

In the kitchen, Mattie found a note propped against the sugar bowl on the table. *Kids, Went to work early. Will be home late. Get dinner and do your homework.*

Mattie frowned. Mama had to work late again. This was the fourth time in the past two weeks. How could Mama do the superintendent chores and work overtime at the factory, too? Eventually Mrs. Rausch, the manager of their building, was going to find out that things were falling apart at 6129 Julian Street. Mrs. Adams was complaining about her dripping kitchen faucet. The Reynolds' radiators didn't work, and old Mr. Richards wanted a new stove. If word got to Rausch, Mama would be in trouble. Rausch the Rat was what Mattie called the real estate agent, but not so anyone could hear.

Mattie poured oatmeal into a pot of boiling water and stirred it furiously. She forced back the tears that came when she remembered how things used to be when Daddy was alive. He would have fixed the faucet and the radiators and ordered a new stove for Mr. Richards.

"And he would kiss me and call me his princess," Mattie murmured. Mama never did that. Mattie ached for her father. She was only eleven and it didn't seem fair that she would never see him again. Daddy had gone to work as usual one day six months ago, and on his way home some drunk driver had hit his car and killed him. From that day everything in her life had changed.

Mattie turned the stove down to simmer and called out to her brother. "Get yourself up, Matt Matisse. I've got the cereal cooking."

Matt hated oatmeal, but she couldn't stand his favorite either — Malt-o-Meal. He wouldn't be happy about the oatmeal but they had agreed that the first one up got to choose breakfast.

Mattie poured the oatmeal into two bright yellow bowls and was already eating when Matt took his place at the table. He groaned when he saw the oatmeal, but that was the only greeting he gave Mattie.

The twins ate silently, cleaned the kitchen, and left for school. Matt didn't even seem to notice the bright sunshine and cotton candy clouds that promised a glorious April day. Mattie hummed to herself as she waited for her brother to speak. When he did, the words fairly exploded out of him.

"Darn it, Mattie. Oatmeal again and I didn't have a clean shirt and I didn't have a chance to tell Mama that the Reynoldses stopped by again yesterday afternoon about their radiators. They want them fixed now," he stormed. Matt was as thin and copper-colored as Mattie, and he had the same large dark eyes.

"Look, Matt, I'll do the wash tonight. Did you tell Mr. Reynolds that Mama put in their request?"

"No, because I don't think Mama did put it in, Mattie. Things are getting worse all the time." Matt kicked at the pavement in frustration.

"Not worse, just the same," Mattie sighed. She watched her brother, knowing there was more.

"Mama won't eat," he continued. "She hardly sleeps. The house is a mess except for the times you clean it. I never know whether she's going to cry or smile or yell. We never laugh anymore, Mattie. We never have any fun. You call this a family?" His brown eyes challenged her.

Maybe it was because they were twins and twins were special, Mattie knew. But they understood one another and fiercely protected one another. Mattie wanted to say something now to comfort her brother, but before she had a chance, her best friend, Toni Douglas, called to them from the corner by her apartment building. Mattie eyed her twin and they silently agreed to erase their faces. She and Matt had always been able to communicate without using words.

"Hey, girl, ready for the math test?" Toni shouted as she waited for them to catch up. She was a bouncy, cheerful girl with bright black eyes and thick black hair that she wore in braids. A fire-engine red beret was perched on the side of her head.

"Well, are you ready?" she repeated, not even noticing when Matt barely mumbled good-bye and walked on. "I did my homework but I just know I'm going to fail. You know what, Miss Mattie Mae Benson? I'm just too young to understand fractions."

Mattie didn't answer. She pulled her thick navy sweater around her shoulders and watched Matt walk away. Her thin brown face would have been unremarkable except for her eyes. Intelligence and caution existed together in those huge brown circles. Mattie was all dark brown eyes and copper-colored angles. Not Toni Douglas. She was a chocolate bubble floating through life.

"Of course you're prepared," Toni went on, ignoring Mattie's silence. "I bet I'm the only one in class who isn't, except for those two dopes, Angel and Charlene."

Mattie groaned when she heard those names. Angel Higgley was the one person in school who gave her trouble, and Charlene was Angel's shadow. If ever anyone was misnamed, Angel Higgley was.

5

I wonder what she's going to try today, Mattie thought. *I'm not going to let her copy off me. Let her start another nasty story about me, I don't care. It can't be worse than the one about me having body odor. That was mean.*

Mattie found Toni's nonstop chatter soothing. It was one of the many good things about her friend. Mattie didn't have to explain herself to Toni and answer a whole bunch of questions. They had started school together and had been friends since that first day.

"So I told Daddy," Toni was off on a new topic, "I didn't want to enter the writing contest. I mean, you know me, Mattie. English is my best subject, but I've already decided what I want to give Mom for Mother's Day. I'm going to make her a shawl. I've picked out the pattern and the yarn." Toni paused to catch her breath.

"Yeah, what does it look like?" Mattie was finally jolted into conversation.

"The yarn is lavender with silver threads running through it. I saw it at Stern's. The pattern is really fancy, but Mrs. Stamps said she'd help me with it. I have the money saved up. Don't you think Mom will like that?" This time Toni waited for Mattie's answer.

"She'll love it. You know how excited she gets over anything you make. Remember those funny-looking pot holders you made for her when we were in second grade?"

They laughed together as they remembered the crazy pot holders Toni had made out of purple cotton loops.

"What's the contest you were talking about?" Mattie asked.

"The one in the *South Side Daily*. Didn't you see it? You have to write an essay about what your mother means to you. If you win, your family gets a dinner 'in one of Chicago's better restaurants' " — Toni repeated the words in the newspaper article — "and 'movie tickets and a copy of *Roots*,' too."

"No money?" Mattie asked.

"Oh, sure. First prize is fifty dollars. Not bad, huh?" Toni came to a sudden stop and grabbed Mattie's arm. "Look, Mattie. He's there."

"Who?" Mattie followed Toni's gaze.

"The new boy, the one who transferred from Ridley School. He sits right across from you. How could you ignore Larry Saunders? He's the best-looking boy in our class." Toni tugged at her braids and adjusted her beret. "Now don't act like you see him or like we've been talking about him," Toni warned.

Mattie smiled at her friend. Toni was practically dancing with anticipation. The girls had to cross the corner where Larry was stationed as a crossing guard this morning.

"If we work it just right," Toni said, "we can get held up by the light. That will give us thirty-seven seconds. Miracles can happen in thirty-seven seconds. Maybe he'll speak to us." Toni clenched her teeth to stop from grinning. "How do I look?" she asked.

"On a scale of one to ten, maybe a three," Mattie teased.

"Oh, no. What's wrong with me? Tell me."

"Nothing's wrong with you. You look fine. I was just teasing. You look better than Angel Higgley."

"Now you are making fun of me." Toni pulled at one of her braids. "She's the best dressed girl in class."

"No, I'm not making fun of you. You're better than Angel any day and anyone with good sense can see that," Mattie declared.

"I hope Larry can see it," Toni said, taking Mattie's arm and heading for the corner.

But when they got to the intersection, Larry was so busy urging a line of straggling children across the street that he just looked back and waved the two girls across.

"Come on," Larry yelled. "Hurry up!"

"Toni, I'm crossing with or without you," Mattie said.

Toni was forced to move. This wasn't the way

she had planned it. She ran across the street, catching up with Mattie as she stepped up on the opposite curb.

"You two are worse than the little kids," Larry glared at them.

Without a word, the two friends hurried away. Toni yanked her beret off and stuffed it in her pocket.

"Who does he think he is?" she sputtered, looking back over her shoulder.

"The best-looking boy in class." Mattie grinned at her friend, and they both broke out in laughter and raced to the school building.

The bell hadn't rung for class yet so the girls leaned into the chain-link fence that surrounded the playground and watched their schoolmates. The concrete pounded with the sounds of double-dutch. At least a dozen pairs of feet hit the pavement in a steady rhythm. Mattie chanted the rope song as she and Toni watched their classmates dash in and out of the swiftly turning ropes.

*Sally Sue went to school early Monday
morning.
Sally Sue went to school early Monday
morning.
Double-down, double-down, double-down,
Sally Sue.*

Double-down, double down, double-down,
   Sally Sue.

When the bell sounded, Mattie and Toni joined the line for their class and waited to file into school.

"So here's the math whiz, Mattie Mae Benson." The voice of Angel Higgley came from somewhere behind Mattie in line. "Bet she's going to get a hundred on the test today. What do you think, Charlene?"

Mattie hunched her shoulders defensively as the taunting words curled around her. She was grateful when the line began to move.

"You bet she is," Toni shouted. "She's going to get another hundred and she's going to sing about it all the way home." Toni knew she had scored. All the kids remembered that Angel had tried out for the lead in the school musical last year and lost to Mattie.

"You've got some things to worry about, Toni Douglas," Angel threatened. "If you don't watch out you're going to lose that funny-looking hat of yours. Too bad you can't lose some of that blubber as easily."

As Angel pushed ahead of her into the classroom, Toni grabbed at the hat that was working its way out of her pocket.

Mattie stared at Angel's sleek pageboy. There wasn't a hair out of place. Mattie yearned to mess it up, twist it until Angel begged for mercy. One rough twist for every cruel word. But her father had told her that fighting was the easy way out. "Stay cool," he had said.

Mattie put her arm around Toni's shoulders. "Don't let her get to you. Angel's the one with blubber."

"Yeah. Where? I don't see it."

"She's got blubber on the brain." Mattie laughed. "See you at recess." She hugged Toni and hurried over to the cluster of desks she shared with Michael, Larry, Charlene, and Angel. When the math test was passed out, Mattie set to work. Daddy was right. If you stayed cool you made it through.

Mattie finished the test before anyone else and turned her paper over on her desk. She reached inside for a book. Out of the corner of her eye she caught Angel's catlike gaze. Her eyes were moving back and forth from her test paper to Mattie's. The meaning was clear.

Mattie jerked her chair back and picked up her paper. Mr. Ashby, her teacher, was monitoring the class from the back of the room. Mattie headed straight for him. Putting the paper into his hands, she reached for the bathroom pass. Mr. Ashby nodded permission.

There was no telling what Angel would do to her for this, but Mattie didn't care. Not too many kids dared to cross Miss Queen Bee. Mattie was angry with the bunch of dopes who always hung around Angel. Girls who wished their eyes were gray instead of black. Girls who dreamed of having long wavy hair like the white girls on television. Girls who didn't realize that they, too, were lovely and special.

When she got back to her classroom, Mr. Ashby was collecting the test papers. Mattie slid into her chair avoiding Angel's eyes. A piece of paper was sticking out of her desk. She reached for it in anticipation, expecting one of Toni's funny messages. But the note wasn't on the bright green paper Toni used.

Mattie sensed trouble. Charlene was watching her over the top of her speller. Unfolding the note carefully in her lap, Mattie read the words: *Trouble is coming your way.* The white notepaper had a skull and crossbones sticker on it.

Without looking up, Mattie pushed the note deep into her desk. Angel was getting even. Should she give the note to Mr. Ashby? The very thought set her heart pounding. She couldn't be a tattletale. Anyway, she had no real proof. It was her word against Angel's. Mattie's stomach knotted. She wasn't a fighter in Angel's league.

TWO

"So, what are you going to do about Angel?" Toni asked.

Recess had just started and Toni and Mattie were walking along beside the fence of the playground, as far from Angel and her crowd as they could get.

"I should go to Mr. Ashby and say — "

"Yeah, say what?" Toni interrupted. "Mr. Ashby, I found this note in my desk, and I know Angel wrote it because I wouldn't let her copy the answers on my math test?"

"That's what I should say," Mattie muttered.

"And what do you think he would say?" Toni demanded. "Angel Higgley, I've had enough of your sneaky ways. You are going to the principal's office?"

"Maybe," Mattie murmured.

"Mattie Mae Benson, you're a dreamer. That's not going to happen. Angel is too smart to get caught. You don't have any real proof. You think that robot, Charlene, is going to tell on her?"

"Well, what am I supposed to do? Turn into a bully like her?"

"You could tell your mother or Matt."

"No, Mama's too upset already. And what could Matt do? I don't want to get him into trouble. No, I can't let them know about this, and don't you say a word. Promise?"

"Okay. Okay. Cross my heart and hope to pass the next math test." Toni grinned.

Mattie stared through the fence at the park across the street. The trees were covered with new green leaves, and fresh spring grass spread over the ground like a rich carpet.

"What are you thinking about?" Toni leaned back against the fence.

"That park is special to me. There are all kinds of trees there — one called the gingko tree from Asia. The leaves are shaped like small green fans. There's only one in the whole park. My father and I found it — I can remember the day.

"Daddy had just come home from work and I was reading a book about Dr. King. I couldn't understand why black people weren't allowed to vote and had to sit in the back of the buses. Daddy took me to the park to talk about it. He didn't even change his clothes before we went — funny what you remember. We found the tree and later I went to the library and found out what it was. Daddy called it our fan tree. It was our special tree." Mattie's eyes filled with tears.

"Don't cry, Mattie. I'll stick by you, and I won't let Angel bother you either."

The rest of the morning passed uneventfully. At noon, Mattie and Toni shared their lunches. On their way back to their classroom, Mattie saw a new, colorful bulletin board display in the hall. It had Matt's artistic stamp all over it.

"Toni, look! Another Matt special."

"He's good all right," Toni agreed. "Your mother must be proud of him."

"I wish she was proud of me. She finds fault with everything I do. Everything!"

"She's just not herself, with your father gone and all. It's not you, Mattie, really. Come on, we have to go. The bell's ringing."

All afternoon Mattie waited, tense and expectant, for Angel to carry out her threat. But nothing happened. When it was time to go home, Mattie gathered her books together. She had to carry all of them home because Mr. Ashby believed in giving homework assignments. As she walked over to get in line to leave, Toni called to her.

"I have to talk to Mr. Ashby about the math test. Wait for me outside."

Mattie left the room and started down the steps, clutching the load of books in both arms. She was helpless when it happened. Someone pushed her — hard. Startled, she let the books fly and grabbed the rail to break her fall. Stunned, she searched the faces around her. There weren't any teachers or monitors in sight.

Mattie looked up into Charlene's wide eyes. She seemed frightened as she thrust a library book into Mattie's hands. "You sure are clumsy, Mattie Benson. Maybe she needs some lessons in walking. Huh, Angel?"

Pulling on her bangs, Angel stared at Mattie. "Or maybe she doesn't understand about notes with skulls and crossbones on them," Angel said.

"You lay one hand on me — you push me again, and I'm going to get you — both of you," Mattie shouted.

"And I'll be right there to back her up." Toni had appeared at the top of the stairs. "Come on, if you two want a fight, let's go."

As Toni started down the stairs, the two bullies ran off, screaming with laughter.

"Mattie, what happened?" Toni asked.

"I was going down the stairs and one of them pushed me."

"Have you got all your stuff?" Toni asked, picking up a stray sheet of notebook paper.

"I guess so. Hey, what got into us? We actually sounded like we were going to fight them. What if they'd taken us up on it?" Mattie giggled.

"I was so mad! We do have our limits though, Mattie. Enough is enough," Toni declared as they left the school building.

"Toni, I've got to hurry. I have to go home and then go to the Bacons to baby-sit. What are you doing tomorrow?"

"I want to go downtown and get the yarn for Mom's present. Why don't you come? We haven't done anything fun on a Saturday in a long time. Let's go together."

"I don't know what Mama will say. I have all this homework to do."

"Mattie, even condemned prisoners feast one last time. We deserve a break. We stood up to the two ghouls. Come on, we'll just be gone part of the day." Toni knew by the slow grin on Mattie's face that she had won.

"Let me clear it with Mama. I'll call you in the morning. By nine," Mattie said, as she ran off up the street.

The lock on the apartment door was stuck and Mattie could hear the phone ringing inside. When she finally got the door open, she ran to the living room and lunged for the phone.

"Hello!" she shouted.

"Well, I was beginning to wonder if anyone lived there. I'd like to speak with your mother," said the irritated voice of Mrs. Rausch.

Mattie tried to get her thoughts together. What should she say? She couldn't use the excuse again that Mama was downstairs doing such and such.

"Is anyone there? I don't have all day to wait. What *is* going on?" Rausch had never sounded so angry before.

"Oh, Mrs. Rausch, I'm sorry to keep you waiting. I just came home and I was looking for Mama's note. It says she's out looking for parts for the stove repairs you approved. Then she'll be vacuuming the halls in the front. Wait, there's a PS. She has to stop by the doctor's to get a prescription for my brother's asthma."

"Asthma? I didn't know your brother suffered with asthma. Your mother never mentioned it. And I thought she located those parts last week. Why is everything so slow there? I'd come over and check for myself but I don't have the time."

"Oh, you don't have to come over," Mattie said quickly. "Everything's fine."

"Well, tell your mother that I'll be in my office briefly tomorrow morning. Tell her to call me at the office at ten-thirty sharp. We have some serious problems to discuss. Don't forget to tell your mother exactly what I said," ordered Mrs. Rausch and then hung up.

Mattie put the receiver down. She crumpled the imaginary note in her hand and tossed it away. Mama was going to be mad. But Mattie refused to think about that now. She had to get ready to go to the Bacons.

When she arrived at the snug, brick house, Cherise was crying and Sharon was fussing because their mother had to leave. Mrs. Bacon, starched and professional in her nurse's uniform, bustled from the front door to the kitchen to the hall closet as Mattie greeted her. Mattie picked up Cherise and handed Sharon an apple from the fruit bowl.

"Mattie Mae, I've got good news for me but not-so-good news for you," Mrs. Bacon said in her no nonsense way. "For the next three months or so, I'll be working days again. I start Monday."

"You mean you won't be needing me anymore?"

"Honey, I couldn't pass up the opportunity to work days. It means more time with my family."

"I understand. That's real nice for you and your family. I understand," Mattie repeated.

"Now, you know we'll call you whenever we go out. Honey, you're the best baby-sitter we ever had. Look, here's an envelope with a little extra money for this week — for all the extras you give us. I know this is sudden, but I was just notified this morning. I hope you'll come and visit us, Mattie. We consider you family. And who knows, I may be back on nights sooner than butter melts in a hot skillet."

Mattie barely heard the door close behind Mrs. Bacon. Maybe seven dollars a week wasn't much to some kids, but it meant five for Mama and two for Mattie. "I've got more than fifteen dollars saved," she said to herself. "I could have gotten Mama something real nice for Mother's Day."

"Mattie, I want to hear the cornrows story," Sharon begged, sputtering apple on her T-shirt. "The one about the girl with hair like mine."

Mattie fingered the colored glass and wooden beads that decorated the elaborate pattern of braids that hung like raw black silk on Sharon's head. She had wondered how Mrs. Bacon made the time, then one day Sharon told her that her father braided her hair.

"Okay, go get the book," Mattie said. "If you listen quietly, Cherise, we'll read one of your favorites, too." Mattie hugged the relaxed two-year-old and sank down with her on the living-room couch.

After three stories, the girls were happy to play with their toys. Before she started her homework, Mattie opened the envelope Mrs. Bacon had given her and counted out ten one-dollar bills. Since her father's death, there was never enough money and everything she earned helped. She'd have to hunt up another job.

By six-fifteen, Mattie had finished her math homework. Mr. Ashby had outdone himself this weekend. His homework assignment included math, spelling, a social studies essay, a book report, and some vocabulary words. He was determined to make his fifth-graders work. And he worked, too. He graded every paper.

When she heard the front door lock turn, Mattie was playing with the children.

"Hi, Mattie, how are the kids?" Mr. Bacon stood in the doorway. When he saw her face, he grimaced. "So Vera told you. I'm sorry, Mattie."

Sharon and Cherise grabbed their father's legs and demanded kisses and hugs. Mattie remembered racing to the door when her father's key turned in the lock. She always had a thousand things to tell him when he came home. Matt would hang back a little, but he always tried to be there to welcome Daddy home. Sometimes he'd put a sketch by Daddy's place at the kitchen table.

Too soon it was time to leave the Bacons. Mattie got her sweater out of the hall closet and then hugged Cherise and Sharon until they squirmed. The pay envelope lay on top of her math book. Stuffing it into the pocket of her sweater, she kissed the girls again and accepted a friendly pat on the shoulder from their father.

"See you, Mattie," Sharon shouted. "See you on the day coming."

"Bye, Sharon. Bye, Cherise." Mattie would miss her visits to the Bacons — and not just because of the money.

THREE

Matt had dinner started when Mattie got home — salad and leftover spaghetti. There was a sheet of paper by her plate. Mattie picked it up and looked over at her brother. But Matt kept stirring the spaghetti on the stove, his back to her. He had drawn a girl with musical notes coming out of her mouth and the notes turned into spring flowers that were sprinkled all over the paper.

"Thanks, Matt. I love it."

"Okay," he mumbled. "Let's eat. I'm starving. I made enough for Mama when she gets home."

"I'm glad you're talking to me again," Mattie said as her brother dished out the spaghetti. "I mean, you were mad this morning."

"I'm too hungry to be mad. Plus I got moved to the top reading group today. Mrs. Collins said if I keep it up, I might make Student of the Month! Did you see my bulletin board? I haven't felt like this about school since Daddy — " He stopped and lowered his eyes.

"Yeah, I know. Sometimes, I expect to see Daddy come through that door and sit down at this table and say, 'Now, Matthew, what went on in school today?' Remember?" she said, touching his arm.

"I remember. What happened to *you* in school today? You look like you lost two best friends." He looked at her as he stuffed a forkful of food into his mouth.

Mattie resisted the urge to tell him about Angel and Charlene. No telling what he'd do and she didn't want him to get in trouble in school. She decided that those two were her problem.

"Mrs. Bacon got put on days, so I'm out of a job. Unemployed. No more five dollars for Mama." Mattie stabbed at the spaghetti.

"Look, Mattie, five dollars a week won't hurt us too much. You'll get another job."

"I just hope we don't have to pay full rent."

"What are you talking about?" Matt demanded.

"Rausch called. She wants Mama to call her first thing tomorrow morning. She sounded mad. She said they have some serious problems to discuss." Mattie imitated the woman's angry voice.

"If Daddy was here she wouldn't talk to us like that," Matt said, tipping his chair back.

"If Daddy was alive, a lot of things would be

better," Mattie echoed ruefully. "Oh, Mrs. Bacon gave me a couple of extra dollars."

Mattie handed her brother the pay envelope and he counted out the bills. "Ten ones and a ten-dollar bill," he said. "Nice."

"What ten-dollar bill? There wasn't a ten-dollar bill when I counted the money!"

"Maybe you have a fairy godmother. Anyway, we can use all the extras we can get." Matt reached for more salad. "Eat. You get skinnier every week."

Ignoring his order, Mattie counted the money again. "It was Mr. Bacon. He must have added this ten while I was getting my sweater out of the closet. That sure was nice of him." Mattie smiled. "Okay, I'll eat, if you leave me some."

"Listen, I think I hear Mama." Matt got up from the table and went over to the stove.

Mattie tensed, waiting. She heard her mother walking down the hallway and then stop. She looked up.

Mrs. Benson was leaning against the frame of the kitchen door. She was a small, tired-looking woman. Wisps of curly hair twisted out of a tight bun at the nape of her neck.

"Mama. Sit down. I'll fix you a plate," Matt offered.

"Not too much, Matt. I'm not hungry." Mrs. Benson sank slowly into her chair at the table. The brown corduroy skirt and yellow sweater that had once fit snugly, hung loosely on her body.

"You got paid, Mattie," she said picking up the envelope. "Good. Now you take this money, and some I'm going to add, and buy yourself some clothes." Mama's eyes rested on Mattie a bit distantly as if she was straining to bring her into sharper focus.

"I don't need clothes, Mama. We need this money for other things," protested Mattie.

"Yes you do, and that's that. Matt and I can handle any problems that come up, can't we, son?" She turned to Matt.

"Sure, Mama, sure." Matt avoided looking at his sister.

"Mama," Mattie began, hesitantly. "Mrs. Rausch called this afternoon. She wants you to call her tomorrow morning at ten-thirty sharp."

The twins watched their mother. The sudden clenching of her hands told them she was upset.

"What did you say to her? Did she ask where I was? What did you say to her, Mattie?" The questions hit Mattie like bullets.

"I just told her that you were out getting cheaper parts for the stove, then you had to do the front halls and get some medicine for Matt." The words ran on like a swollen mountain stream.

Mrs. Benson's face clouded with anger.

"Cheaper parts! I called her this week and told her I found the stove parts. The man is coming tomorrow. I told you that, Mattie. What in the world do you use for brains?"

"But I didn't know, Mama. You didn't tell me."

"Are you talking back to me? Are you telling me that I can't remember what I say from one day to the next?"

"No, Ma'am." Mattie drew back, her eyes pleading with Matt for help.

"Come on, Mama. Don't get upset. Mattie just said what I would have said. Except for the part about my being sick." He grinned, trying to lighten the tense mood in the kitchen.

"What is this about medicine for Matt?" Mama asked, relaxing a little.

"I told her he has asthma." Mattie said warily.

"Having me get asthma is a great idea." Matt laughed. "I mean how can Rausch tell if I do or not? And you can say that you had to return those stove parts because they weren't in good shape. She's not going to put us out," he said with more conviction than he felt.

Mrs. Benson propped her head up with her hands. "Things feel like they're falling apart all around me. Something's always wrong. Something always needs fixing," she said.

"Mama, eat something," urged Matt.

Mrs. Benson ignored the food. She picked up Mattie's pay envelope and took out the money.

"Mattie, why is there so much money here?"

"Mrs. Bacon got changed to days, so they don't need me anymore. They gave me some extra." Mattie felt the food lodge in her throat.

"Charity! That's what this is! We are not taking charity! Just because Vera Bacon has a husband, she thinks she can dole out charity to me and mine!" Mrs. Benson twisted her wedding band around and around.

"It was Mr. Bacon. He put the ten dollars in! I didn't know anything about it until I got home," Mattie explained.

"Mama, you're getting mad about nothing," Matt said. "They know what a good baby-sitter Mattie is, and they felt bad about not needing her. Look, you're tired. Eat a little and lie down. We'll clean up."

"I'm not hungry. I'll lie down for a while." She got up, leaving the plate of food.

Mattie sat at the table with tears streaming down her face while Matt cleared the table, then disappeared into his room.

Mattie got up and washed the dishes. Then she put a load of clothes in the washing machine in the basement. She moved back and forth quietly past her mother's closed bedroom door. Two hours later, she had dried the clothes, straightened up the apartment, and said good-night to Matt.

She climbed into bed and stared at the pale space

on the wall by her bed, where one of their family pictures had hung. Mama had removed all of the pictures, and the spaces were like wounds on the wall.

Mattie lifted the corner of her mattress and pulled out a photograph wrapped in one of her father's handkerchiefs. There was Daddy with his arm around a happy Mama, and Mattie hugging him around the waist. Mattie touched the joyful faces that Matt had photographed.

She put the picture under her pillow. Thoughts of her father, gingko trees, and silky fan leaves of rose and mauve floated through her mind. She pushed her mother's angry face away and thought of better times when she was Daddy's girl. Finally, she fell asleep.

FOUR

Mattie was searching for the telephone on the playground. It kept ringing and ringing, drowning out Angel's shrill laughter. Finally, Mattie woke up and realized that the telephone wasn't in her dream. Hopping out of bed, she scrambled into the living room.

"Hello?" Mattie yawned, wondering who could be calling so early, and on a Saturday morning.

"Can you go? Did she say yes?" Toni's excited voice crackled over the phone.

"What time is it?" Mattie asked, trying to focus her eyes.

"It's eight-thirty. I couldn't wait for you to call. Listen, I can be at your house before ten. We'll be back by one. I promise. See you soon."

Before Mattie could reply, Toni had hung up.

"Who was that, Mattie? Not Mrs. Rausch I hope?"

Mama's voice preceded her into the living room. Tightening the belt to her jeans, she waited for Mattie's reply.

"Good morning, Mama. No, just Toni. She wants to get some yarn for her Mother's Day gift, and she asked me to go downtown with her. She says we'll be back by one. Is it okay if I go?"

"If you clean the apartment when you get back. Matt and I can do the halls and the steps. Maybe you could pick up any trash in the courtway." Mrs. Benson sank into the chair across from Mattie and rubbed her temples.

"Headache, Mama?" she asked.

"I've had this one for six months," Mama said, more to herself than to Mattie. "Look, I want you to take the money I'm going to give you, add it to the money you got yesterday, and buy yourself some clothes when you're downtown."

"Mama, I don't want any clothes."

"You may be clean and neat, but you look like an orphan. I really ought to go with you."

"Oh, Mama, can you?" Mattie's face brightened.

"I'm afraid not, Mattie. I've got to deal with Rausch. You go on. But don't buy me any Mother's Day present. I don't want anything. Do you hear me? Nothing! You spend that money on school clothes." Mrs. Benson pushed herself out of the chair. "I need some coffee," she sighed.

"But we always celebrate Mother's Day," Mattie protested.

"Not this year. You heard me. No presents!"

Mattie watched her mother walk into the kitchen. Maybe Matt was right, they weren't a family anymore. Last Mother's Day Daddy took them all out to dinner and Mama laughed, and kissed them when they gave her their presents. I always got kissed last, Mattie remembered, but at least I got kissed. Now she never kisses me.

An ache brewed in Mattie's stomach as she dressed. She stole a long look at her father's picture before she put it back under the mattress and made her bed. It would be nice to be needed again, for Mama to say, "Mattie, I need you. I love my daughter." How could Mama refuse to celebrate Mother's Day?

The train ride downtown and Toni's happy chatter helped push the disappointment of the morning aside. Sunlight glared on the dirt-streaked windows of the Jackson Park El. Mattie patted the coin purse in her coat pocket as she watched the apartments and houses of the South Side of Chicago flash by. She had thirty dollars in her purse. Mama had stood over her while she counted the money and tucked it in her purse. Her orders were clear.

"Nothing for me! Nothing for Matt! You hear me?

You come home with some decent clothes. The next time I see that red shirt, it had better be in the garbage!"

Mattie touched the collar of her shirt. Daddy had bought it for her. She would never throw it away. She wondered how Mama could forget. She looked over at Toni who was pulling a magazine out of the large plaid tote bag at her feet. "I want to show you the shawl I'm going to make." She flipped through the magazine until she found the picture, then she held it in front of Mattie.

"Toni, that's beautiful!" exclaimed Mattie, taking the magazine. "I love those lacy edges."

"That's the shell stitch. I had to spend a lot of time practicing with Mrs. Stamps before I could get it right. She's awful nice. She always asks for you, Mattie. Why don't you go and see her anymore? She misses you." Toni thrust a small ball of yarn into Mattie's hands. "This is the yarn I'm going to use."

Mattie held the ball of yarn up to the window so that the sunlight sparkled on the silver threads. The yarn was light and incredibly soft. Mattie held it to her cheek.

"Toni, I never saw yarn with silver in it. Where did you find it?"

"Shopping with Mom at Stern's. I sure was lucky to have some money with me. You know me, by Wednesday my allowance is gone with the wind —

or with cheeseburgers and candy. But I had three dollars left, enough for one ball. Girl, I've washed dishes, baby-sat my brother, taken out the garbage, ironed, scrubbed floors, anything to earn enough money to buy this yarn. Mom thinks I've gone crazy," Toni said proudly.

"I would have lent you some money," said Mattie, returning the yarn and the magazine. "I know you'd pay me back."

"Mattie, I know that. But Mother's Day is different. I want to pull this off all by myself." Toni looked into Mattie's eyes. "You understand?"

"Hey, I do," said Mattie. "I understand. You do this your way." She squeezed Toni's hand.

The girls swayed far to one side as the train rounded a wide curve. Below them were large empty lots strewn with bottles and papers. In the spring morning they had a neglected, abandoned look, as if no one cared about them or the people who lived on their borders. Soon the alleys and backyards of the South Side were behind them as the train sped downtown.

Mattie's pulse picked up as she and Toni got off the train and headed for Stern's. When they entered the polished revolving doors of the store, they stepped into another world. Men and women strolled up and down the aisles with purpose and confidence. Perfumes and colognes mingled in a heavenly aroma. Bouquets of spring flowers decorated the counters. Mattie was enraptured as she inhaled the world of the secure and the wealthy.

Toni headed for the elevator, pulling Mattie along behind her. She pressed the fourth floor button with calm assurance. Mattie counted five black customers and three black saleswomen, but Toni acted as if she weren't counting anyone.

"After I get the yarn, we can look for clothes for you, okay?" offered Toni.

"I can't buy anything here. This stuff must cost a fortune," Mattie whispered, not wanting to attract attention.

"How do you know? You haven't even looked. Anyway, they have a budget floor. I bet we can find something there. Come on, we get off here."

"How do you know all this?" Mattie asked as she followed Toni over to the yarn and fabrics department.

"Because Mom shops here. She says that most of the stores where we live sell cheap products for expensive prices and you might as well come down here and shop the sales. Now help me find Lavender Mist, Number 251, Dye Lot 12C," Toni said, taking the ball of yarn out of her tote bag.

A young saleswoman smiled at the girls and nodded toward the bins of colored yarn. "Can I help?" she asked.

While Toni talked with the saleswoman, Mattie

walked around the tables of fabrics, running her hand over the bolts of soft silks and bright-colored cottons. She imagined herself dressed in a long silk-and-satin gown " . . . and I'll wear a diamond crown with my braids," she giggled.

"I found it!" Toni came toward her hugging the bag of yarn. "I've got more than enough to finish the shawl, and the saleslady suggested that I crochet a handbag to match. She found a pattern for me — all shell stitches! Wait until Mrs. Stamps sees that! Now for your clothes," she said, ignoring Mattie's protests.

Toni expertly guided them down the escalators to the basement. Expecting some dismal hole, Mattie was surprised to see wide aisles and even some smaller bouquets of flowers.

"Come on, I know where your size is," said Toni, threading her way through the racks of clothes. "What do you want to get?" she asked.

"I don't know? *I* don't want to get anything. This is Mama's idea."

"Maybe a couple of blouses, or a pair of jeans and a skirt will satisfy your mother. How much money did she give you?"

"Ten dollars."

"Mattie, tell the truth. Your mama would never send you out shopping for clothes with only ten dollars. How much?" Toni repeated patiently.

"Thirty dollars, but I can't spend it all."

"Thirty plus the five I owe you. Here it is," said Toni.

"No. You might need it," Mattie argued.

"Then I'll earn some more. Here, now I don't owe you. Thanks for not charging interest." Toni laughed.

"I've been saving, too, but I can't think of anything special to give Mama. She doesn't want anything but I have to make her see — "

"See what?" Tugging at one of her braids, Toni held up a skirt she had taken off the rack.

"Just make her see that we should celebrate Mother's Day," Mattie finished, lamely.

"If you go home without any new clothes, she's going to celebrate on you. Come on, I can't shop if you won't cooperate."

Finally, Mattie agreed to try on some clothes while Toni hunted over the floor for bargains. She had the instincts of a born shopper. After an hour and a half of hard work, Toni was satisfied. She had found Mattie a light blue T-shirt, a yellow blouse with blue flowers on it, a pair of yellow jeans that had some torn loops, and a navy blue cotton skirt. Only thirty-two dollars! Mattie couldn't believe how much they had bought, and how good the clothes looked — not thin and flimsy like the clothes in Hudson's Bargain Store on 63rd Street. Mattie felt exhilarated in spite of herself. She grinned at Toni.

Toni smiled back, joy spilling over her like too much root beer in an ice cream float.

Mattie gazed down. The dark brown script letters on her shopping bag stood out boldly, proclaiming that she was carrying purchases from Stern's. Mattie couldn't wait to get home and try the clothes on all over again. Toni had worked out four different combinations of outfits and they all looked good. Mattie decided that Toni was absolutely brilliant!

Enjoying herself now, Mattie stopped to look at some of the merchandise displayed on the first floor. Perfumes, sweaters, belts, handbags with initials, stockings, and jewelry. She turned over the price tag on a red belt she thought her mother might like.

"Twenty-five dollars!" she exclaimed, not caring who was listening.

"Yeah. This isn't the basement. Things cost a lot on this floor. But it's fun to look," said Toni, taking Mattie's arm and heading over to the jewelry counter.

After staring at the rings and bracelets, Mattie bent down to see the pins — emeralds, diamonds, pearls, and stones of all colors and shapes. In the corner of the bottom shelf, she saw a pin so lovely that she caught her breath. It was next to a cluster of pearls set in silver.

The saleswoman behind the counter was black

and this gave Mattie the confidence to speak up.

"Excuse me, ma'am."

"Yes, what is it?" The woman peered over her half-glasses at Mattie and Toni.

"I'd appreciate it, ma'am, I mean, this one," pointed Mattie.

"You mean you'd like this pin?" inquired the woman. Her name badge read, MRS. GROVER.

"She means that she would just like to look at it," Toni explained hastily.

"This pin is expensive," warned Mrs. Grover as she bent down to unlock the glass case.

Mattie continued to stare as the saleswoman placed the pin in the center of a black velvet pad on the counter. The pin looked small and fragile against the dark backdrop. Its single creamy pearl glowed richly.

"Look, Toni, how the gold twists," said Mattie.

"That's called filigree," Mrs. Grover told them. "You have good taste for someone so young."

"Thank you, ma'am. I've never bought any jewelry before." Mattie's voice was hushed with the wonder of what she had found.

"Well, good taste is expensive, as you will learn. This pin sells for fifty-five dollars. But considering the price of gold, you're getting a good buy. Shall I gift wrap it for you?"

"Uh . . . Uh . . ." Mattie stammered.

Ignoring the knowing look in Mrs. Grover's eyes,

Toni pulled Mattie back. "You want that? Who for?" she demanded.

"For Mama. It's just perfect. That's the gift I've been dreaming about. But what can I do? I don't have a job anymore and I don't have that much money."

"I've got ten dollars left. We can put a hold on the pin and then try to figure out how to come up with the rest of the money."

Toni dug into her overflowing bag and pulled out a coin purse shaped like a flower.

"Girls, I have other customers waiting." Mrs. Grover's long dark fingers tapped impatiently on the glass countertop.

Slowly, Mattie went over and touched the pin. As she lifted it up, her fingers felt warm. The pearl rested among the braids of gold like a miniature moon.

"My circle of gold for Mama," murmured Mattie.

"Miss, do you want it?"

"Yes, I do!"

The woman's surprised expression was not lost on Mattie.

"But I don't have the money with me today."

"Then you can't take it with you, I'm sorry." Without another word, Mrs. Grover put the pin back and relocked the case.

"On this piece, you'd have to leave a deposit of at least twenty dollars and pay the balance in thirty days." Mrs. Grover's eyes blinked rapidly over her glasses.

"I only have ten dollars with me, but I have more at home."

"Ten is not twenty. When you have twenty dollars, you can place a hold on the pin." Mrs. Grover moved over to wait on a stout man who was growing restless.

"But what if it's not here when I get back?" pressed Mattie.

"Excuse me a moment, sir?" Mrs. Grover came back to the anxious pair. "Girls, I've tried to help, but there is nothing more I can do. When you have twenty dollars, I can hold the pin for you for thirty days. Now, please."

Her face softened a bit when she saw Mattie drop her head.

"It's likely the pin will be here when you return," she said. "This is a simple piece, somewhat old-fashioned. Most customers prefer something more modern and ornate. Now I'm sorry, but I must wait on this customer," she said, moving away.

Toni tried to console Mattie as they walked toward the door. "There are plenty of other things just as nice that you can give your mother. What about the red belt you liked?"

"Why don't you enter that essay contest instead of making the shawl?" countered Mattie.

"I get your point. Then we have to figure out

some way to get the money. You got enough saved up to hold it, right?"

"Sure, in my sock. But I don't have enough to buy it," moaned Mattie. "I wish I could return these clothes!"

"Don't you dare! I'll kill you! I never shopped so hard in my life. Anyway, you can't take them back, they were on sale. Look, I'm hungry. Let's get something to eat and talk this over. My treat."

"But what if the pin is gone when I come back next Saturday?" Mattie wailed.

FIVE

An hour later, Mattie ran into the apartment. Toni was at Stern's keeping an eye on the pin, and Mrs. Grover. Mattie ran toward her room and collided with Matt in the hallway.

"What did you buy?" Matt asked when he saw the shopping bag.

"Matt, I've got to hurry and get back to Stern's. I found this great pin for Mama. But don't tell her," Mattie said. "These are new clothes. Don't tell Mama I came back. I have to go right back to Stern's. Toni's waiting for me."

"Rausch gave Mama three weeks to shape up or lose her job," Matt said, following Mattie into her bedroom.

"But Mama *is* doing her job. That Rausch! Mama's doing too many jobs — that's the trouble."

"Rausch doesn't care about that or about us.

Anyway, I tried to calm Mama down. I told her it was just one of Rausch's scare tactics. But you know how Mama is lately." He waved his arms in the air.

"Where's Mama now?" asked Mattie, counting out her money.

"She's sweeping the landings and steps in the back. She wouldn't let me. She said it helps work off her anger. I have to go collect on my route now. See you later. Good luck!" He gave her their thumbs-up sign and left.

All the way back downtown, Mattie kept her hand on the coin purse. "I sure hope Toni can protect Mama's pin. Mama's pin." Mattie smiled. She knew Matt would never give her secret away.

When she got back to Stern's, Toni's wide grin told her that the pin was still there.

"Here it is. Twenty dollars," said Mattie, handing the bills to Mrs. Grover. "Now no one else can buy the pin, right?"

"That's right. For thirty days. I'll write out the sales slip and give you the pink copy. Don't lose it. You'll need it when you come back for the pin," explained Mrs. Grover.

Mattie searched the case. The pin wasn't there. "Where is it, Mrs. Grover?"

"Right back here." The saleswoman picked up a small blue box that had been hidden away and opened it. The pearl glowed.

"You mean you put it away for me?"

"I'm not supposed to, but my instincts told me that you'd be back with the deposit. And your friend *was* standing guard."

They all laughed, but Mattie's heart sank when she saw the balance due within one month. She hadn't realized the tax would be so much.

"Some way I'll get the money," she vowed as they left the store.

On the ride home, Mattie was absorbed with plans for earning the money, and Toni concentrated on the pattern instructions for the handbag. When they reached Toni's building, Mrs. Stamps called out to them from her third floor window.

"Come up and have a cup of tea. Both of you. I've been watching for you. No excuses now! Hannibal and I are waiting."

The girls waved at her and went up. Mrs. Elvira Stamps' apartment was as crowded as an antique shop. A small stone Buddha sat in one corner surrounded by potted plants. China cats, dogs, elephants, girls with parasols, and boys with pails crowded the shelves. Lace doilies covered the backs and arms of every piece of furniture.

"The tea is all ready, and I made lemon cakes this morning," said Mrs. Stamps, carrying a lacquer tray loaded with good smells.

"Now sit yourselves down and tell me what you've been up to. Hannibal, no tea for you. Down!"

She gently pushed her German shepherd away from the table.

Mrs. Stamps was a wonderful listener, clapping and crowing at the right moments. The colored stones in her rings flashed as she waved her hands and served the tea. There was nobody like Mrs. Stamps. She wore a long scarlet-and-orange caftan and several necklaces and long earrings that dangled and tinkled when she moved. Hannibal lay at her feet like a patient protector.

"But there's a money problem," Toni explained. "Mattie needs about forty dollars to get the pin."

"And I only have thirty days," said Mattie, biting into a lemon cake.

"That is a lot of money. What are your plans?"

"I don't know," Mattie confessed.

"Maybe Matt could help you out. Then the gift could come from both of you." Toni suggested. "You did that last year."

"No. It's got to be from me. Just me."

"Sounds like this is more than a Mother's Day gift," commented Mrs. Stamps.

"Well, things aren't so good at home. Maybe Mama would feel better if she got something special," said Mattie.

"This pin must be wonderful. You're expecting it to do quite a bit," said Mrs. Stamps.

"If I could get another job. Or borrow the money

and pay it back later. Maybe I can win the money," yelled Mattie, jumping up and startling Hannibal.

"It's all right, Hannibal," crooned Mrs. Stamps. "Let's not get carried away, Mattie. I've been waiting for over forty years for the Million Dollar Man to knock on my door but so far only the bill collectors have come." Mrs. Stamps smiled as she rubbed her dog's back.

"The essay contest!" Toni exclaimed. "You could enter, Mattie!"

"What contest?" asked Mrs. Stamps.

"The one in the *South Side Daily*," Toni told her. "If you write the best essay about what your mother means to you, you can win fifty dollars."

"It's a long shot," said Mrs. Stamps, "but I don't see how you can earn forty dollars baby-sitting in one month, Mattie. The contest is at least a possibility."

"Not for me it isn't," said Mattie. "I can't write fifty-dollar essays. I can't write fifty-cent essays. Toni can, but not me. Why aren't they having a singing contest? I might win that."

"You could try," Toni insisted. "I've got the rules downstairs in my room. I'll go get them. You can do it, Mattie, smart as you are," urged Toni as she ran out of the room.

"Mattie, how do you know what you can do until you try?" said Mrs. Stamps. "If you live your life based only on what you think you can do well, you won't achieve very much. Your mother means a lot to you, so you've got a headstart."

"I really want to give her the pin. But I'm no writer, Mrs. Stamps. I wish I was," sighed Mattie.

"At least try. Maybe Toni could help you. What other choices do you have?"

"Not any, unless I rob a bank," replied Mattie. "And that's not going to happen."

Toni entered the room like a fast-rolling ball. "Here it is. You can write a draft like Mr. Ashby taught us. Then I'll read it over and help you."

"And I'll supply the tea and cookies to fuel this adventure," said Mrs. Stamps, as the little clock on the side table chimed two o'clock.

"Oh, no, I told Mama I'd be home by one. She's going to be mad."

"Then hurry home," Mrs. Stamps said quickly, going to the door with Mattie.

SIX

Encouraged by the support of her friends, Mattie put the contest form on top of the books on her desk when she got home. Then she dragged out the vacuum cleaner and started to clean the hall.

Mattie hadn't gotten as far as her mother's room when she heard the front door open and saw Mama push her way into the apartment and slam down a bucket and mop.

"Mattie, you were supposed to be home over an hour ago. Where were you?"

"I'm sorry, Mama. I forgot to watch the time."

"Forgot to watch the time! What if I forgot to watch the time!" Mama was yelling.

"It won't happen again," Mattie said softly. "I just forgot."

Her mother's hand reached out and Mattie felt the full force of the slap across her cheek. "Maybe that will help you remember your responsibilities!" stormed Mrs. Benson.

"You hit me, Mama. You hit me. Why?" Mattie's voice was growing louder with each word. "Why are you so mean to me? You're not mean to Matt. I'm yours, too, Mama," cried Mattie. "I was just a little late, that's all."

Mattie took off for her room and slammed the door, not caring what her mother did. Her cheek smarted from the slap, but a place inside of her hurt more. The contest form on the pile of books mocked her. This was the first time anyone had slapped her. Her father had never hit her. One look from him was enough to insure obedience.

The door of her bedroom opened. Warily, she looked up. It was Matt.

"What's going on now? Mama's in there crying. You're in here crying? What happened to your face?" He touched her cheek gently.

"Mama hit me," replied Mattie, pushing his hand away. "I was over an hour late because I was trying to figure out how to get the money for her Mother's Day present," said Mattie with a bitter smile. "When I got home she started yelling, and then she hit me. Slapped me."

"Oh, sis." Matt sat beside her on the bed.

"Matt, I know she loves you best, but she didn't have to slap me."

"She loves both of us," protested Matt. "You

have to stop thinking that she doesn't love you."

"Matt, I know the truth and so do you." Mattie went to the bathroom and ran some cold water over a washcloth.

"Mattie, let me do that." Mama was standing in the doorway.

"I can do it." Mattie bent her head to the washcloth.

"Mattie, I didn't mean to hit you." Mama sat on the edge of the tub. "I'm sorry."

Mattie said nothing. She held the cool washcloth to her cheek.

"Honey, I love you. I said I'd never slap a child of mine, and I did. What's happening to me?" She reached out to her daughter.

"It's okay," replied Mattie, not looking at her mother.

"No, it's not, but I don't know what to do." Mrs. Benson withdrew her hand and got up. She walked back to her bedroom and shut the door.

Mattie went back to cleaning the apartment. After mopping the kitchen floor, she asked her mother if she could go to the drugstore to get some writing paper. It was just an excuse to get out of the apartment. Mrs. Benson nodded.

Mattie considered going to see Toni, but the cheerfulness and the warmth of Toni's family would be too much for her to handle right now. She had forty minutes before she was expected back home. As she stared up at Toni's building, she remembered someone who would want to see her. Carefully, she pressed the bell and smiled when Mrs. Stamps answered.

"I was just fixing a snack for Hannibal," the old woman said, as she opened the door to Mattie. "And a cup of tea for myself. Won't you join me?" she asked, realizing something was wrong.

"Yes, thank you," replied Mattie, bending down to rub her cheek against Hannibal's face.

"He's really taken with you, Mattie, and Hannibal is an excellent judge of character." Mrs. Stamps led the way to the kitchen. "Now you sit there and tell me what happened."

"Mama got mad and . . ." Mattie touched her cheek.

Mrs. Stamps clucked several times and then disappeared. She returned with a small white jar in her hand.

"Just the thing to soothe that cheek. It won't hurt." She spread ointment over Mattie's cheek and kissed her. "Now, that should feel better. Doesn't it?"

Mattie nodded.

"Nobody ever slapped me before. I was late and she got furious." Mattie started to cry as she relived the ugly scene. "Why, Mrs. Stamps? Why is she so mean to me?"

"Your mother is under a lot of pressure. She's not herself, child," consoled Mrs. Stamps as she busied herself making tea.

Her kitchen was as crowded as her living room. Potted plants filled the counters and hung from hooks in the ceiling. Rows of spice bottles lined the shelves above the stove. The air was always full of baking smells and roasting smells.

"She said she didn't mean to hit me," Mattie admitted grudgingly.

"Honey, I know your mother. I knew your father. Your mother is a good woman. She's just got too many things happening too fast right now and she feels that there's no one to help her — "

"I help her! Matt helps her! I'd do anything she asked me to," interrupted Mattie.

"I know. I know. But she always had your father to depend on and now she has two children to raise alone, and on one salary," explained Mrs. Stamps, putting the teapot down on the table and taking Mattie's hand.

"I miss Daddy, too. So does Matt. Things were good when he was alive. Now it's all bad."

"No, child. Nothing is ever all bad. I think your mother needs to talk to someone, to help her through this hard time. The pastor, or a counselor," suggested Mrs. Stamps, thinking aloud. "These are the times to hold on to your faith. This is when loving your mother really counts."

"I'm scared of her," Mattie confessed. "She's always angry or crying."

"Well, maybe thinking about the gift will help you. Have you decided to enter the contest?"

"After what happened?" Mattie bit her lip.

"Well, you think about it," Mrs. Stamps urged.

Twenty minutes later, Mattie was almost home when she saw Charlene coming toward her, struggling with three bulging pillow cases that Mattie guessed were full of laundry. Charlene was having a difficult time holding on to all of them. Two of the pillow cases dropped and soiled clothes tumbled out all over the sidewalk. As she scurried to pick up the laundry, Charlene began to cry.

"I'll help," said Mattie, rushing over.

"I can do it." Charlene sniffled, wiping the tears away. "I don't need your help."

Mattie looked at Charlene's thin face and worn jacket. She had seven brothers and sisters and her family was ten stops past poor.

"Yes, you do," Mattie argued, stuffing clothes into a pillow case. "Why didn't one of your brothers or sisters help you carry these?"

"It's none of your business. Anyway, this is my job. I've got to go," Charlene said, barely managing to hold onto the laundry.

Mattie took a deep breath. "Hey, I'll carry one," she offered.

For a second Charlene's expression softened. Then she squared her shoulders.

"No, thank you. I can do it," she insisted.

Mattie watched Charlene struggle off. The Laundromat was four blocks away.

Mattie entered the hallway of her apartment as quietly as she could. Matt was in the living room watching television.

"Hi, how are you doing?" he asked.

Mattie shrugged. "Where's Mama?" she asked.

"Fixing dinner. I already set the table and made a salad. Toni called for you," he said.

"I'd better check with Mama before I call her back." Mattie headed for the kitchen.

"Mama, can I help?" she asked as her mother moved from the sink to the stove.

"No," said Mrs. Benson. Then, seeing Mattie's face drop she said, "Watch this pot while I change my shoes, okay?" Lightly she touched her daughter's cheek. "Maybe we could go to a show tomorrow," she said. "Like we used to."

"That would be nice, Mama." But Mattie didn't plan to count on it.

When the telephone rang in the living room, Matt called his sister. It was Toni again.

"Well, did she like the clothes? What about the yellow jeans and matching top?" Toni bubbled.

"I didn't get a chance to show her yet."

"What's wrong?" Toni asked.

"I'll talk to you tomorrow after church, Toni. Thanks for all your help today."

Later that night, Mattie sat at her desk and reread the directions for the contest. She took out a sheet of paper and began writing. After balling up several sheets and throwing them into the wastebasket, she turned out the light and got into bed. She pulled the covers over her head. She would never be able to write a winning essay.

SEVEN

At breakfast the next morning, Mama said she had a throbbing headache. She would not be going to church and she was sorry but the show that afternoon was out. Mattie watched Matt try to hide his disappointment, but said nothing.

"Maybe we can go next weekend," Mama said. Her eyes rested on her son's face. "Matt, I'm sorry. I'm just not up to it." With that she got up, leaving the plate of food she had prepared.

"Well, no use sitting here," said Mattie. "I sing a solo today, so I'd better be on time."

"How's your cheek?" asked Matt, as he helped Mattie clear the table.

"It's okay." Mattie felt self-conscious. She wanted to forget the incident that had humiliated her so.

"Mattie, what are we going to do? Mama's getting worse, not better," said Matt.

"I know. I talked to Mrs. Stamps," Mattie confided. "She says that Mama needs to talk to someone, Reverend Harris or a counselor. She says that Mama is under too much pressure."

"But how are we going to get her to talk to some-one? You know how she is."

"Search me. Why don't you talk to her?" Mattie suggested. "She listens to you. She won't pay any attention to me."

"I don't know. I never can figure out her moods. But I'll try," he promised.

Mattie wore her new blouse and skirt to church. It cheered her up and she knew it would please Toni. She and Toni sang in the junior choir, but Toni dashed in, late as usual, so they didn't have time to talk. After church, they chatted while Matt was talking with Reverend Harris.

"Can you come over today?" asked Toni. "I asked Mom and it's okay. She's waiting for me."

"I think so. Mama's got another headache. So she's not cooking."

"You can come for dinner then," Toni said. "Say, what was the matter with you when I called last night?"

Mattie frowned. She hated to lie to Toni, but this wasn't the right time to explain. "Mama was upset, that's all." Mattie was relieved to see Matt coming toward them.

"Hi, Toni."

"Hey, Matt, want to come for dinner, too? Mattie's coming. You can take a plate home to your mother."

"No thanks, Toni, I've got some drawings I want to finish." He gestured for Mattie to come with him and she told Toni she'd see her later.

"So what did you say to Reverend Harris?" Mattie asked as soon as they were alone.

"We just talked a little. He said he would call Mama later today. Mama respects him. I hope he can help."

"So do I. He *has* to help her," said Mattie.

"Don't set your hopes on it," he cautioned.

When they got home, the apartment was quiet. Matt peeked in his mother's room. She was asleep. After he and Mattie straightened up the kitchen, she told him she was going over to Toni's. She took a notebook, pencils, and the contest form.

Mattie decided to stop in the drugstore on the way and buy Toni some pretzels. As she stood in front of the potato chips and pretzel display, she heard Angel's hateful voice.

"Charlene, look who's out. I didn't know bookworms came out on weekends, did you?"

Mattie looked around. Ignoring Angel, she asked, "Did you make it to the Laundromat all right, Charlene?"

"Yeah, I told you I would," said Charlene.

"My daddy bought us a new washer and dryer,"

boasted Angel, and then cruelly turned on her friend. "Charlene, you didn't even comb your hair this morning. And it looks dirty."

Nervously, Charlene picked at her hair as Mattie pushed past them.

"I haven't forgotten about you," Angel called after her.

Mattie came back and faced her tormentor. "Look, you. I don't know why you keep bothering me, but I'm not afraid of you." Mattie was surprised at her own strong response.

"I just don't like smart girls like you who know all the answers and don't share them," said Angel. Her eyes were piercing and mean.

Mattie turned away again, paid for the pretzels, and left the store.

Working with Toni on the essay wasn't any fun. Mrs. Douglas' ample Sunday dinner had settled comfortably in Mattie's stomach and all she wanted to do was snuggle up with a good book.

"Let's try another approach," said Toni. "I'll write and you talk. Tell me everything that comes to your mind when you think about your mother."

Toni sat on the bed cross-legged, with a pencil poised over a blank sheet of paper.

"Tired, mad, sad, and more tired," Mattie recited, not lifting her head from the pillow.

"Go on."

"Beautiful when she smiles. Always has a headache. Real careful about doing things right. Likes the smell of freshly washed clothes and Daddy's after-shave. I mean she used to. Loves pretty jewelry, mint ice cream, Agatha Christie mysteries and . . ." Mattie stopped.

"And . . ."

"Matt." His name filled the room. "And me, sometimes. Toni, do you think I'm going to have to give up the idea of getting that pin for Mama?"

"I don't know. I hope not, but maybe it's not the gift for her. I mean, there are a lot of other things you could get her. Why not two gallons of mint ice cream?"

"Toni, stop it. I'm set on the pin. It's *the* special gift. I have to get it for her. Get out another sheet of paper, and let's try one more time."

But after another hour of fruitless struggling with the essay, Mattie and Toni decided to give up and try another day.

As Mattie headed home, with two carefully wrapped plates of food for Matt and her mother, she thought, *What a family Sunday — me and Toni's family.*

Before she could get her key in the lock, the door was pulled open. Matt hushed her and waved her into the hall.

"Listen, Mama's mad. Reverend Harris came by to talk to her, and she says I betrayed her. You go right to your room," he whispered urgently. "I'll take the food."

Mattie was handing him the food as her mother came out of her bedroom.

"You two get in here!" she ordered, clutching her worn robe closer. She slammed the front door and marched into the living room. "What do you mean talking to Reverend Harris about me? I know Matt did the talking, but you put him up to it, didn't you, Mattie? Tell me the truth."

"No, Mama, I mean, Mrs. Stamps said that it might help," pleaded Mattie.

"And when did that old fool start running this household? I didn't know she had a degree in psychology. You went outside this family and told our business, Mattie. I should whip you for that."

Matt moved between his mother and his sister.

"Mama, stop it. You're ready to hit Mattie again, when all she tried to do was help you. We didn't know what to do," Matt was shouting now.

"When did you start talking to me like that?" Mrs. Benson was genuinely shocked. "You'd better watch your mouth. And you, Mattie, don't you dare go out of this family with our troubles again."

"Mama, I didn't mean to upset you. I just wanted you to feel better. Mrs. Stamps said you were under too much stress and pressure."

"I don't want to hear what that woman thinks," Mama said. "What I need is Rausch off my back and some money." Mrs. Benson went back into her bedroom and closed the door.

"What do you think, Matt?" sighed Mattie. "Did we make it worse?"

Matt looked at his sister and shook his head. "I don't know what to think."

EIGHT

On Monday morning Mr. Ashby went around the room handing back the math tests. Toni was groaning and holding her head down on her desk, waiting for her paper. Angel cut her eyes at Mattie as Mr. Ashby put her test paper down in front of her.

"This was a very important test, Angel," he said. "You got the lowest score in the class. Didn't you study? Were you ill?" Mr. Ashby sounded concerned. "I thought you'd do better. Your father said you were studying harder."

"I felt sick to my stomach on Friday. Could I please take it over, Mr. Ashby?" Angel pleaded.

"No. If I let you take it over, I'd have to let others take it over. You'll just have to do better next time. Toni, you did better than I expected."

Toni's grin lit up the room, and she waved her paper at Mattie.

"Well done, Mattie." Mr. Ashby dropped the paper on Mattie's desk and moved on.

"My father promised me five dollars if I got a good grade," Angel hissed. "Even dummy over there got a better score than me." She was pointing at Charlene. "You'll pay for this, Mattie Benson, you'll pay."

Mattie got up and went to the bookcase. She needed to put some space between herself and Angel. Out of the corner of her eye, she saw Angel take Charlene's paper and begin to copy off it and erase her own paper.

During recess Mattie managed to avoid Angel. But when she returned to her desk later, her heart dropped — another note with a skull and crossbones. Scrawled words filled the page, as if someone were deliberately trying to disguise the handwriting, but Mattie knew.

WINNERS, LOSERS, LOSERS, WEEPERS. YOU LOSE!

When Angel casually sauntered to her seat, Mattie stiffened. Delicately, Angel arranged the folds and ruffles of her pretty skirt. Then she took out her pocket mirror and checked her hair.

"Angel, this is not the bathroom," Mr. Ashby reprimanded.

"Oh, excuse me, Mr. Ashby," she murmured, masking her glower with a false smile.

"I know you wrote this note, or put Charlene up to it," said Mattie quietly.

"I don't know what you're talking about." Angel turned away.

"Yes, you do," insisted Mattie.

"Mattie, you have work to do," said Mr. Ashby.

"I'm going to tell him if you keep this up," Mattie whispered.

"You don't dare," Angel said. "Anyway, you don't have any proof."

"I'll get the proof," Mattie retorted.

"Mattie! Angel!" Mr. Ashby ordered them to be silent, and for the rest of the day they avoided one another.

When Mattie got home after school, she changed her new clothes for old jeans and a sweatshirt. After sweeping the kitchen floor, she began grating cheese for a macaroni and tuna casserole. She was putting the leftover cheese back into the refrigerator when she heard her brother's step in the hallway.

"Hey, twin!" Matt was beaming when he came into the kitchen. "I get to move to the top math group like you. Start calling me Matt the Brain. You know," he said, "this school thing isn't all that bad. Daddy would be proud of me."

"He sure would be. It was important to you, wasn't it?"

"What?"

"Daddy being proud of you."

"I had Mama on my side, but more than anything I wanted Daddy. I knew he loved me and all, but you were his favorite," said Matt.

"He talked about you all the time — and about us, the family. He had plans for us," said Mattie.

"You never told me that."

"You never seemed interested. I always felt that you had Mama and I didn't." Mattie didn't add that she still felt that way.

"You've got to get straight about Mama — she loves you, Mattie. You've got to stop brooding about it. Which reminds me, there's something I've been meaning to ask you."

"What?"

"Late at night, when I check the apartment, I go by your room and the light is still on. I can hear you muttering and fussing in there. What are you doing?"

Mattie opened a can of tuna and began to flake it into a bowl.

"I'm trying to write something, and it's hard."

"What is it? Or is it a secret?" Matt asked, leaning back against the kitchen sink.

"I don't want you to laugh at me and say I'm being silly," said Mattie as she concentrated on her cooking.

"I promise not to laugh. Come on," he urged.

"It's an essay contest. The one in the *South Side Daily*. If I write an essay about what Mama means to me and win first prize, I get fifty dollars."

"With fifty dollars you can buy a lot," he said.

"I can buy that pin I told you about. I can give it to Mama and then she'll know," said Mattie.

Matt frowned. "What is that pin going to tell her that she doesn't already know?" he asked.

"Matt, this is very important to me. Sometimes I worry that Daddy never knew how much I loved him. I know that Mama doesn't love me as much as Daddy did" — Mattie went on despite Matt's angry protests — "but if I could give her this pin, maybe she'd know and things could be better."

"I think that's silly, Mattie. Well, not silly, but a pin can't fix what's wrong with this family."

"Maybe it can fix the way I feel," yelled Mattie. "I want to give her that pin."

"Okay, okay. Don't get excited. Mama yelling, and now you yelling. I'm tired of all this yelling!"

As they stared at one another, they heard a key turn in the front door lock.

"Matt, Mattie, come and help me," called their mother.

Matt ran down the hall and caught one of the grocery bags their mother was carrying before it hit the floor. Mattie grabbed for the other one, but missed. Cans rolled across the floor.

"Mattie, hurry up and get that stuff up. I have to

work the late shift tonight." Mrs. Benson bent down to pick up a loaf of bread.

"Sure, Mama," said Mattie.

"Did you wear those clothes to school?" her mother asked.

"No, I changed when I got home. I'll get this," replied Mattie, picking up the torn bag.

Mrs. Benson hung up her coat and riffled through the mail on the telephone table. "Bills, nothing but bills. I can't work enough jobs to catch up," she said. "There's never anything nice in the mail for me."

Mattie ducked past her.

"See, who'd she get angry at? Not you — me," whispered Mattie as she put the cans on the kitchen table.

"She's just tired. She gets mad at me, too. Stop making a mountain out of a molehill," Matt grumbled and stalked off to his room.

Mattie put on the kettle and slid the casserole into the oven. When the water boiled, she made a cup of tea and brought it into the living room.

Her mother was sitting on the sofa. She looked so small and unhappy that Mattie felt a heavy sadness for her. When Mama looked up, there were tears in her eyes, but she smiled when she saw the teacup.

"Oh, thank you, Mattie."

"I put the food away, Mama, and dinner will be

ready in about thirty minutes," said Mattie, handing her the cup.

"Come, sit by me," invited her mother.

They sat in silence until Mrs. Benson spoke.

"Mattie, I'm sorry for hitting you and screaming at you. Reverend Harris is right. You and Matt are right. So is your friend Mrs. Stamps. I do need to talk to somebody." She sighed and rubbed her forehead. "I'm so tired, always so tired and worried."

"Mama, I — "

"Now, don't *you* cry. No sense in two of us crying. What's Matt going to think?" She touched Mattie's arm. "I'll rest here until dinner is ready. Thanks for the tea, honey."

That night, Mattie sat at her desk, writing the same sentence over and over again. The essay was headed nowhere. She just couldn't get the right words down on paper. What could she do? A plan began to form in her mind. It was risky, but it might work. Anything was worth making Mama feel better. Shaking away her doubts and bad feelings, Mattie went into the living room and picked up the phone.

"Toni, I need your help. You know you said you would help me write the essay."

"Sure, Mattie, you know I will."

"Well," said Mattie slowly, trying to pick the right words.

"Just tell me," said Toni.

It was harder than she had imagined to win Toni over to her plan. Mattie had to tell her everything that had been going on with her mother for the past several months. Only then would Toni agree, but Mattie knew she didn't like it. When Mattie hung up the phone, her hands were sweaty.

As she counted the money in her sock that night, Mattie was aware of Mama's bedroom down the hallway. So far, she hadn't lined up any new baby-sitting jobs, but Mrs. Stamps had offered to pay her a small sum for walking Hannibal on the weekends. She was a long way from the money she needed, and time was running out.

Mattie lay awake most of the night. The quilt was too warm and heavy. She threw it back and sat up. The small room seemed to close in on her. "If only Daddy were here, he'd understand what I have to do," Mattie reasoned out loud. But she knew that he'd never approve of her plan. Grimly, Mattie turned on the light and checked the clock. Three o'clock in the morning. Mattie paced around the bed. She took out fresh paper and sharpened three pencils. She'd try again.

Morning dawned cool and clean. Mattie saw the sun rise and realized that Mama would be home soon. Stretching to ease the cramp in her neck, she read what she had written. The sunshine crept over the windowsill as she folded the sheet of paper. She slipped it into an envelope, addressed the envelope, and put it in her notebook. She was asleep before her mother came home.

When the twins left for school that morning, Mama was sleeping. Toni was waiting for Mattie by the mailbox and her glum face made Mattie feel guilty.

"Look, I don't like this," Toni said as soon as Matt had walked on. "But I'll go along with it because you're my friend and you need help."

Mattie had never seen Toni look so serious before. "Maybe I won't need it. I mean — "

"Look, girl, I did it and it's good. Take it," Toni said, thrusting an envelope into Mattie's hand. "It's done. Let's just hope this works. We'll know in a couple of weeks."

"Yeah, right."

The envelope in Mattie's hand felt as heavy as a bar of lead.

NINE

Mattie and Toni continued to school in an uneasy silence. Part of Mattie wanted to give the essay back — part of her couldn't.

As they neared the playground, Mattie saw Angel's crowd grouped around her, *oohing* and *aahing*.

"My father gave it to me last night, for my birthday," Angel was saying, dangling her wrist in front of the girls. "These are real pearls on a real fourteen-karat gold chain — not gold-filled. My father said it cost a lot of money. I shouldn't have worn it to school — he told me not to — but I had to let you see it. Especially you, Charlene."

Charlene's face was solid with envy and longing. All of the working and saving in the world would never get Charlene a bracelet like Angel's. Mattie knew it, and so did Angel.

"Would you let me wear it, just at recess?" asked Charlene.

"Wear my birthday bracelet! You'd get it all dirty! But you can touch it," taunted Angel. "Mattie, don't you want to touch it?" She shook the bracelet in front of Mattie's face.

"No."

"I know you don't have a father to give you presents," Angel sniped. "I can understand why you'd be jealous."

Before Mattie could answer, the bell sounded and they had to line up for class. During the morning, Mattie forgot about Angel and her bracelet. But she couldn't dismiss the two envelopes tucked into her notebook. When the lunch bell rang, Toni left while Mattie sat at her desk eyeing her notebook. Angel was still at her desk and Charlene was waiting by the door. Mattie ignored them. When she got up to get her sweater, Angel was gone. Mattie bumped into Charlene as she left the coatroom.

"I forgot my jacket," Charlene mumbled.

Mattie just nodded. When she joined Toni in the cafeteria, she found her friend quiet, almost sullen. Mattie wiped her hands on the sides of her jeans, not sure whether to sit down. What could she say?

"Toni, if you don't want me to send in your essay, I won't. I haven't made up my mind, and I did write something."

"I've never done anything like this before," Toni

said. "But you're my best friend. I know how important that pin is to you. No, you keep it and mail it in," she said, biting into a peanut butter sandwich. "You'll have a chance to win."

"I wish — "

"I wish we'd never gone to Stern's," Toni burst out, and without finishing her lunch she got up and left the cafeteria alone.

Mattie forced herself to go through the motions of eating. When she walked out onto the playground, she noticed for the first time that morning that it was raining. The kids would be in the gym, but she didn't feel like going there. Instead, she returned to the quiet classroom and read a book at her desk. The stillness of the room was calming.

When the bell sounded for afternoon classes, Angel rushed into the room and started digging in the back of her desk.

"It's gone! My bracelet is gone!" screamed Angel, tossing books and papers on the floor. "I didn't want to scratch it at lunch, so I wrapped it in paper and put it in the back of my desk. It's not there!"

"Oh, no, Angel," said Charlene.

"What?" said Mattie, shocked.

"Don't act so surprised, Mattie Mae Benson. We both know who stole my bracelet. You did. You're the only one who saw me put it in my desk!" accused Angel, grabbing at Mattie.

"A fight! A fight! Get her, Angel! She stole it!"

shouted Charlene, jumping up from her seat. Toni moved in to help Mattie.

"What's going on in here?" Mr. Ashby demanded as he entered the room.

"Mattie started it, Mr. Ashby. She stole my bracelet, and then she pushed me. Charlene saw it all, didn't you, Charlene?" Angel whimpered.

"Mattie started it!" Charlene told the teacher.

"Mattie?" he asked, looking at her.

"I didn't steal anything, and she pushed me first," argued Mattie.

"Angel?"

"She was the only one in the room when I hid my bracelet in my desk. Nobody else knew."

"What do you say about that, Mattie?"

"Yes, I was in the room, but I didn't pay any attention to her. I had other things on my mind. I didn't steal her bracelet," Mattie repeated.

"I want everybody in his or her seat," the teacher ordered. "And I mean now!" The class obeyed. Only Toni, Charlene, Angel, and Mattie stood frozen like players in a tag game.

"You four, outside in the hall!"

"I saw Mattie hit Angel," declared Charlene, as soon as they were all standing out in the hall.

"And you, Toni, what did you see?" asked Mr. Ashby.

"I didn't see that part. But Angel has been picking

on Mattie for a long time. Mattie's no thief." Toni defended her friend.

"The real issue is the bracelet. Angel, how can you be so sure Mattie took it?" asked Mr. Ashby.

"She was the only person in the room when I put it in my desk. The only one. Plus, she's been picking on me. I know she wanted my bracelet," stated Angel.

"No, I don't, and I didn't see her put her bracelet anywhere. I don't care about her dumb bracelet," stormed Mattie.

"We'll have to search the room," Mr. Ashby said.

But the room search didn't turn up the bracelet. Mr. Ashby questioned their classmates, but there were no clues. The bracelet had disappeared. At the end of the day, Mr. Ashby told Angel and Mattie to wait after class. He gave each of them a note to take home. There would have to be a meeting with their parents, he said. *Oh, no!* Mattie thought, *what would Mama say!*

Walking home alone, Mattie stopped at the mailbox in front of Toni's building. She took the two envelopes out of her notebook. What should she do? She had to act today if her entry was going to get to the newspaper before the contest deadline. Mattie took a deep breath and pulled back the handle of the mailbox. Her choice slid down the dark opening. It was too late now to change her mind.

She wished that she felt better as she continued home alone.

"Mattie, I'm in here. Where's your brother? I thought he'd be home by now," called her mother as Mattie entered the apartment.

"He'll be home soon, Mama. He has to deliver the papers. What's the matter? You look sick," said Mattie, dropping her books on the living-room table. Her mother was lying on the couch.

"I have another of those horrible headaches." She rubbed her forehead and closed her eyes.

"I'll get you some aspirin and make you some tea," said Mattie.

"I already took two pills. Why were you looking so upset when you came in?" asked Mrs. Benson, raising her head gingerly.

"I wasn't, Mama."

"I know you better than that. Something's bothering you."

Mattie decided to tell her mother about the bracelet, leaving out nothing. Then she gave her the note.

"So, did you take it?"

"Mama! I don't steal. I wouldn't steal. How could you say that to me?" Mattie ran to the bathroom and locked the door. She sat down on the toilet seat and sobbed. The whole day had been just too much for her and now this.

"Open the door, Mattie, please."

Mattie opened the door.

"Oh, honey, I'm sorry. I know you didn't take that silly girl's bracelet. I don't know what got into me, saying something like that to you. Don't cry," Mama said. "I'll call your teacher and I'll ask for a half day off to go to school." She opened her arms to Mattie.

"Mama, I didn't take it. I swear. Please believe me," cried Mattie, hugging her mother.

"Baby, I do, I do. Now come on. We could both use a cup of tea."

When Matt came home an hour later he, too, acted edgy. While he and Mattie heated some leftovers for dinner, Matt confided in her. He kept his voice low.

"I might lose my paper route. Circulation is down and they might be cutting back some of the routes. I tried Smith's Drugstore and the grocery store to see if they needed any help. No luck."

"Don't worry. You don't know for sure you'll get cut. You're the best in the neighborhood."

"Yeah, well, I hope they think so. Why are *you* looking so down?"

"Angel accused me of stealing a gold bracelet her father gave her for her birthday," Mattie sighed.

"She what? I'll take care of her!" he said, banging a plate down on the table.

"Shh . . . Mama's going to talk to Mr. Ashby. *I* know I didn't take the bracelet and so does Mama," said Mattie. "But I wonder who did."

"Listen, if you need any help with that girl, you just whistle." Matt grinned at her as he did his gangster imitation.

They ate dinner together while their mother slept. About eight-thirty, Toni called.

"How did it go when you told your mother about Angel's bracelet?" she asked. "Remember, I'm on your side."

"Thanks, Toni. I told Mama. She believes me."

There was an awkward silence, then both girls started talking at the same time.

"Toni?"

"Mattie?"

They giggled with relief.

"Toni, I want to tell you about the essay — "

"No, don't talk about it, Mattie," Toni pleaded. "It's done and I don't want to talk about it. Let's just see what happens."

"But — "

"I'm serious. Nothing more about the essay. Now we have to do something about this lie Angel has started. She's lying — I'd bet on it," Toni declared.

"No, I don't think so," Mattie argued. "I've been sitting next to her since September and I know her pretty well. She was really upset. Anything her father gives her is special. She may hate me, but I don't think she'd get in trouble with her father. No, somebody stole it."

"She'd do anything to get you, Mattie! She's tricky."

"I know, Toni, but I don't think this is one of her tricks."

"Look, I don't agree," said Toni. "So let's work out a plan to find out which one of us is right. We have to clear you."

"You got any ideas?"

By the time the conversation ended, the friends had forged a scheme to discover the real thief, or expose Angel if this was one of her nasty tricks.

After she hung up the phone, Mattie went into her room and got undressed for bed. The bedside lamp cast a soft glow in the room. The warm spring air through the partially open window smelled of hope and new promise.

Sometime during the night, Mattie woke up. As she made her way down the hall to the bathroom, she opened the door to her mother's room and looked in. The moonlight fell around the sleeping shape of her mother like a cashmere shawl. Mattie looked closer. Mama was wrapped in Daddy's good coat. Her father had worn that coat to church every chilly Sunday. Mattie stepped back into the hallway and closed the door quietly.

"Mama, it's worth anything to give you that pin," whispered Mattie. "Anything!"

TEN

The very next morning, Toni put their plan into action. When Mattie arrived at school, she saw Toni talking with Charlene, but Angel was nowhere around. Mattie stood alone, watching Toni and Charlene line up to jump double-dutch. If she hadn't known better, Mattie would have said Toni was having a good time.

After lunch, Mr. Ashby told Mattie that her mother had called him and that the meeting with the Higgleys would be held as soon as Mrs. Benson could get time off from work — maybe next week. Mattie was relieved, for she and Toni needed time if their plan was going to work.

For the rest of the week, Mattie stayed by herself at school while Toni spent all her free time making friends with Charlene. It was easy because Angel was out sick. But on the following Monday, Mattie watched Angel enter the schoolyard and flounce her way angrily across the playground. Her shrill voice carried across the yard.

"What are you doing talking to her, Charlene? I heard you've been hanging around with Toni. What's the matter with you?"

"She's all right, Angel. Toni doesn't like Mattie anymore. You should hear her talk about Mattie! Makes *you* sound like her best friend," gushed Charlene.

"A leopard changing her spots?" Angel challenged. "What are you trying to pull, Toni?"

"Listen, things have changed between me and Mattie. She's not my friend anymore." Toni sounded very convincing.

"Seems strange to me," Angel said suspiciously. "Last week you jumped into the fight, and now you and Mattie aren't friends?"

"I wasn't fighting you, Angel. I was just trying to keep Mattie from scratching your face all up — like she told me she was going to do some day." Toni watched Angel cringe and stroke her cheek.

"She said that?" Angel stared over at Mattie.

"You bet she did." Toni nodded emphatically.

"Humph, we'll see. Won't we, Charlene?"

"Yeah, Angel. I think Toni's one of us."

"I'll decide that, Charlene. I'm the boss, and don't you forget it," warned Angel. "I know Mattie took my bracelet and she's going to pay for that."

"She hasn't said anything to me," Toni said hastily. "But if she does, I mean if I find out anything, I'll tell you."

It had been fairly easy for Toni to win over Charlene, but Angel was going to be more difficult. Toni felt guilty about using Charlene but it seemed the only way to get to Angel. Toni took a deep breath and started again.

"Angel, I want to invite you and Charlene over to my house on Saturday night. Just food and fun and some good music."

It took a little persuading, but Angel finally agreed to come. Charlene was no problem. She was so eager to have a friend.

Mattie kept an eye on the trio at school and Toni called every night to report on her progress; still, she missed the contact and fun of a school day with Toni.

In the middle of the week, Mattie decided to go to her special place away from home and school. She dug into her pocket and counted out the change. It was enough for the bus to the park. The ride took longer than she'd remembered, but once there Mattie hurried toward the gingko tree she and her father had discovered two years ago.

Mattie spread her sweater under the tree and sat down. A sense of peace quickly enveloped her. Folding her arms to pillow her head, she lay back and watched the clouds as they floated overhead.

She and her father had pretended that the clouds were people heading for faraway places. Smiling to herself, Mattie decided that the cloud-people were bound for Dar es Salaam.

Mattie rolled the word on her tongue. Visions of dusky-hued women wrapped in scarlet, gold, and ivory-colored cloth filled her head. She imagined she could even hear their beaded headdresses tinkling as they glided through the centuries-old markets amidst modern skyscrapers.

"There I am, just like Daddy said, an African princess, a lovely African princess, carrying the leaves of the gingko tree like a dozen golden fans on top of my head."

Humming softly, Mattie sat up, reached in her back pocket, and unwrapped her favorite photograph. She had decided to carry it with her today, and her father's strength seemed to reach out and hold her.

When Mattie finally got home from the park, the apartment was deserted. There was no note on the kitchen table and no Matt. After putting the photograph back under her mattress, Mattie started dinner — chili, rice, and salad.

While she was setting the table, the phone rang. It was a baby-sitting job — the Wagners who lived across the street. Mama wouldn't mind that on a school night and it would mean more money toward the pin. The phone rang again, while Mattie was eating dinner before going to the Wagners. It was Matt saying that he'd stayed late at school for basketball tryouts.

It was almost six o'clock when Mattie heard her mother's step in the hall and the key turn in the front door. Where had Mama been? Mattie helped her mother with her light coat, knowing better than to ask any questions.

"Mama, I was worried about you."

"I had something to do. You get dinner started?" she asked. Her fingers rubbed the edge of the sofa.

"Yes. It's all ready. Can I fix you a plate and bring it to your room?"

"No. I don't have much of an appetite yet. Maybe I'll eat later. Where's Matt?"

The same old question: Matt? Matt? Matt?

"He called. He stayed late for basketball tryouts. Want some tea?"

"Honey, that sounds good," sighed her mother, reaching out to pat her hand. "Mattie Mae Benson, you are a good daughter."

Mattie grinned. Humming, she made the tea, placing the teapot and mug on a blue tray. She was determined to hold onto the good feelings she had found under the gingko tree.

"My, that dinner smells good. Did Mrs. Rausch call?" Mama asked, sipping the tea.

"Nope, not a word from her. Can she take your job away, Mama?"

"Yes, she can. Maybe working two jobs is too much for me. Any more trouble about the bracelet?"

"No. But they still want that meeting as soon as you can make it," said Mattie.

"I'll make it. Don't you worry about that. I got permission to take half a day off next Monday. I'll call Mr. Ashby."

"I'm glad. Everybody thinks I stole it."

"Well, you didn't, and we'll get this straightened out. Why do you still have on your school clothes?"

"Oh, I have a baby-sitting job tonight," explained Mattie.

"You seem to be doing a lot of baby-sitting. We don't need money that much. I want you home on school nights," answered her mother. "Every time I turn around you are going off to baby-sit for somebody."

Mattie didn't know what to say. She changed the subject quickly, before her mother started talking about money. "Okay if I call Toni?"

"Yes, but don't talk too long. I think I'll lie down until Matt comes home. I'll send him over to the Wagners when you're ready to come home. Call first. I don't want you out alone late. Do you hear me, Mattie?"

"Yes, Mama." Mattie dialed Toni's number as soon as her mother left the room.

"So, what's new with the two ghouls?" asked Mattie when Toni came to the phone.

"You know, Mattie, Charlene isn't so bad. She just needs to be . . ." Toni hesitated. " . . . cared about, I guess. It's not just that she's so poor — nobody seems to care about her."

"Yeah, I know. But why does she hang around with that nasty Angel?"

"I think Angel is lying about the bracelet being stolen. I really do, Mattie."

"No. Somebody took it, Toni. Angel is too upset. I don't think she's pretending this time."

"Angel hates you, Mattie. She doesn't like anybody else much either, except for Larry. She and Charlene are coming over on Saturday night. Angel fell for everything. All you have to do is adore her and she likes you."

"We didn't plan that! Why did you ask Angel?"

"I want the two of them together. Maybe something will slip out. Maybe Charlene knows where Angel put the bracelet, or maybe Angel will say something."

"Oh, Toni, this sounds like a lot of maybes. I'm going to Stern's on Saturday and stopping in to see Mrs. Stamps. I wanted you to come with me."

"I wish I could, but with those two coming over, Mom wants me to clean and shop with her," said Toni.

"What are you going to do with them on Saturday?" asked Mattie.

"Listen to music and talk. I figure I have to get those two talking. Charlene hasn't said anything but I think she knows something."

Mattie heard the front door open and close and watched Matt dribble an imaginary basketball into the living room and shoot a basket into the far wall.

"Listen, Toni, I've got to go now. I've got a baby-sitting job tonight, and I go to the Bacons on Saturday. I'll talk to you in church on Sunday."

"Oh, no, Mattie. I can't talk to you in church in case they see me. Meet me at Mrs. Stamps' after church."

"Okay." Mattie hung up the phone and looked at her brother. His eyes were shining.

"I made the basketball team *and* I get to keep my paper route." He grinned happily.

"*All right!* Why didn't you say something before about basketball?" she asked.

"I had to decide if I wanted it. Being on the team means I can't be home so much," he said.

"But I can help Mama, if that's what you're worried about. Say, Matt, do you know where Mama was this afternoon?"

"No. Why?"

"I'm not sure. She came home late again and there wasn't any note. She seemed different — not so angry."

"Well, good, Mattie. That's nothing to get upset about."

"Yeah. Hey, I've got to get to the Wagners'. Mama said to call when I'm ready to come home. You'll come get me, okay?"

"Okay, little sister." Matt hadn't been this happy in months.

Mrs. Grover wasn't at the jewelry counter on Saturday afternoon. A young salesgirl behind the counter explained that Mrs. Grover was on her break, but that she could show Mattie the pin if she had some proof of identification. Mattie handed over the pink deposit slip, and a few minutes later the girl returned with the pin.

Mattie held her breath. The pin looked lovelier than ever. She took out the nine dollars that she had saved and held it out to the salesgirl. But she would not take it. She had to have all of the money, the girl explained. Mattie groaned. She'd hoped that she could add a little money every time she'd earned some.

"I can only accept the balance."

"But I don't have the balance yet," Mattie said.

"Well, when you do just bring it in. No problem!" assured the salesgirl. "They'll hold it for you for thirty days."

Mattie stuffed the bills back into her purse and carefully folded the pink slip.

On her way home, she buzzed Mrs. Stamps' bell twice, and got a quick response. One nice thing about Mrs. Stamps was that things stayed the same. There was tea and lemon cake slices and soft music playing. And her friend listened attentively as she talked.

"The salesgirl said I couldn't put any more money on the pin until I had it all. I'm twenty-five dollars short and I have just a little over three weeks to get it," said Mattie mournfully.

"What about the essay contest?"

"I sent one in, but I haven't heard anything yet. Nothing at all. Did Toni say anything to you about it?" Mattie asked warily.

"No, she hasn't said anything. I'm sure you worked hard on that paper, and as much feeling as you have for your mama, I just know that things will work out," said Mrs. Stamps.

"I don't know, Mrs. Stamps. I hope I win. I can't explain it, but I know that pin will make things better in our family."

"That pin is not going to solve all your family's problems," her friend warned gently.

"Why not? Mama will know I love her and how special she is," argued Mattie.

"But your mother's problems are bigger than that, honey. She has to learn to take care of her family by herself. I'm not saying that the pin won't help. Just don't expect it to work miracles," cautioned Mrs. Stamps.

"You mean I shouldn't try to give her that pin?" asked Mattie.

"No, I'm not saying that. But a gift is more precious when you just give it and don't expect something in return," she said. "What would happen if you weren't able to buy the pin?"

"I'd want to die," Mattie declared. One look at Mrs. Stamps' face convinced her to change that statement. "I was just saying that. I don't know what I'd do. Give her something else, I suppose. But it wouldn't be the same."

"You have to accept the fact that you might not win the contest."

"I have to win. I took a big chance and I have to," Mattie burst out, waking up Hannibal, who jumped up and started barking.

"It's all right, Hannibal. Mattie is just excited," soothed his owner. "Mattie, you may be letting yourself in for a big disappointment. On the other hand, this may wind up being the triumph of your young life. You have to accept the risks."

Sharon and Cherise jumped all over her when she arrived at the Bacons' at seven o'clock.

"They miss you, Mattie." Mrs. Bacon touched Mattie's shoulder fondly. "Every day they ask for you. Mr. Bacon and I had no idea you and the girls were this close."

"That sure is the truth. There's only one baby-sitter for us, and that's you, young lady," echoed Mr. Bacon.

"A Saturday night out on the town! What a treat. We'll be out late, so you go to sleep when you're ready. There's plenty to eat in the refrigerator. Why am I telling you all this? You know this house as well as we do." Mrs. Bacon laughed.

By nine o'clock, Mattie had settled the little girls with a promise that she would be there in the morning. Unable to concentrate on her homework, she shoved the books aside and turned on the television. But she couldn't concentrate on the movie, either.

I wonder what's going on at Toni's, she thought. *I hope she finds out who stole that bracelet. Mr. Ashby has to have real proof before he'll believe me.*

The pin. That's what she had to focus on. She had to practice seeing it come to her. Focus on the positive and work toward it. Mattie reached for the blue pillow on the sofa and lay back, just as the phone rang.

"Mattie?" the voice whispered.

"Who is it?"

"Toni, you dummy. Who else would be calling

you up like some silly spy." Toni tried to muffle a giggle.

"What's going on?"

"I don't have much time. They think I'm in the kitchen getting some more soda and chips. Those two eat like horses! I wanted to tell you — "

"What?" Mattie could barely hear Toni.

"Wait a minute. I think I hear someone coming."

"Toni, what did you find out?"

"I can't talk anymore. I'll see you tomorrow at Mrs. Stamps' — got to go — right now."

What had Toni called to tell her?

ELEVEN

"You two want to go to a show later this afternoon?" Mama asked as they were walking home from church the next day.

The twins exchanged a surprised glance. "Sure," they both replied.

"Good. Pick one out. We'll go around four," said their mother.

"Mama, can I go over to Toni's? Just for a little while?" asked Mattie.

"Yes, I guess so. And, Matt, you finish your homework and whatever secret project you've got back there."

"Mama! You didn't look, did you?" Matt's face was anxious.

"No, I didn't," she said with a smile.

* * *

Mattie climbed the three flights of stairs up to Mrs. Stamps' and started talking the minute her friend opened the door.

" . . . and then Toni called but she had to hang up before she could tell me anything . . ."

"What a mystery!" Mrs. Stamps said excitedly. "Come on in."

When Mattie had finished explaining why she and Toni were meeting at Mrs. Stamps', she felt a need to unburden herself about the essay, too. But before she could finish, Mrs. Stamps held up her hands to stop her.

"Mattie, from all I know about you, I think I can guess which essay you mailed in."

"But I want to tell you."

Mrs. Stamps smoothed the soft folds of her emerald green dress. "Mattie, whatever you decided is done. You have to live with the consequences. If you made the right decision, though, you may be in for some good, skin-stretching times."

"Skin-stretching times?" queried Mattie.

"Yes. Like the creatures that grow by stretching their old skins until they drop off, leaving better-fitting new skins underneath. You want to do that, child?"

"I guess I do," replied Mattie.

"A chance to stretch your skin is rare, Mattie. Most folks feel safer stuffed in old, too-tight skins. It's better to grow, Mattie, inside."

A series of loud knocks on the hall door interrupted their conversation. Hannibal was immediately transformed from a loving pet to a growling watchdog. Mrs. Stamps got up and peered through the peephole.

"Toni, come in," she said, opening the door. "My, you're all out of breath."

Hannibal, once again the loving pet, began licking Toni's hand.

"Hi, Mrs. Stamps, Hannibal, Mattie." Toni nodded to each of them in turn.

"Something to drink?" asked Mrs. Stamps, pouring out a glass of lemonade.

"Oh, please, anything cool." Toni gasped and sank into a large fan-shaped chair. When she had swallowed half the lemonade in the glass, she turned to Mattie.

"It's just like I told you — I mean *tried* to tell you last night. You were right. As hard as it is for me to believe, somebody really stole Angel's bracelet. That's all she talked about last night. A real exciting party."

"It wasn't me," declared Mattie.

"Oh, silly, I know that. But Angel doesn't. Whoever stole that bracelet knew she was going to leave it in her desk. I figure it had to be one of her friends. But she swears that she didn't tell any of them."

"The sad thing is that misfortune is often brought

on by the people closest to us," mused Mrs. Stamps. "We'd like to believe that our pains and disappointments are the work of strangers, but more often than not they are the doings of someone we know."

"Right, Mrs. Stamps. My sentiments exactly!" Toni nodded knowingly.

"I can't bear the suspense any longer. Come on, Toni. Do you know who stole it?" Mattie pleaded.

"*I* don't *know*, but I think it was Charlene." Toni almost whispered the name.

"Oh, she couldn't have," Mattie argued. "She's Angel's best friend. She hangs onto Angel like a second skin."

"Yeah, I know that. But remember what Mrs. Stamps just said, and you haven't been with them," said Toni.

"I have. I sit at the same cluster with both of them," Mattie pointed out.

"That's not the same as being with them away from school. You should hear the way Angel treats Charlene. It's worse than what we've seen. She makes fun of Charlene's clothes, the way she looks, how poor she is — and she acts as if it's a big joke. I'm sure it's Charlene. The problem is how to prove it."

"She could have seen Angel hide the bracelet," Mattie relented. "She was waiting by the door, and

I bumped into her when I was coming out of the coatroom."

"See!" Toni grinned. "Mattie, Angel called Charlene dumb, stupid, stinky, and ugly all in one night. She laughs at her. She won't even let Charlene complete a sentence. Charlene's got the motive. I just have to prove it."

"That won't be easy, if you're right," Mrs. Stamps warned. "Sounds like this Charlene is a pretty torn piece of spirit. She may admire Angel as much as she hates her. For her to steal the bracelet could destroy their friendship and that would be a big chance for Charlene to take. It's not going to be easy to prove."

"And we don't have much time. The meeting with Mama and the Higgleys is tomorrow," Mattie told them.

"You'll just have to hang in there," Toni told her. "They don't have any real proof against you. Give me some time and I'll make Charlene talk if I have to hit her!"

Seeing the horrified faces around her, Toni laughed. "Come on, I wouldn't really hit her," she said, reaching for a slice of lemon cake.

Explaining that she and Matt and Mama were going to the movies, Mattie thanked Mrs. Stamps for her kindness and left the apartment. She ran all the way home.

"Matt? Mama? I'm back," she called.

Matt hurried down the hall.

"Shhh, Mama's got another headache. I guess the show is off."

"Oh, Matt, and I ran all the way home," sobbed Mattie, feeling like a balloon losing air.

"I know. I feel bad, too." He turned and went back to his room.

Mattie sighed and flicked on the television. She didn't hear her mother come into the living room.

"Did you decide on a show?" she asked.

"Mama! Matt said you had a headache and the show was off," said Mattie, getting up.

"No, I made you two a promise and I'm going to keep it. Now, go tell Matt to get ready. We're going to a show and I'm going to take two aspirin," she announced.

It was like old times standing in the popcorn line in the movie theater and fussing about how close to sit. Mattie sat on one side of her mother, Matt on the other, and after the show they went for hamburgers. Mattie couldn't quite believe all the fun they were having. Matt winked at her. Mama was actually laughing.

The meeting with the Higgleys ended in a draw. Mama fought them on every point, establishing Mattie's innocence, or, at least, the lack of any real solid proof against her.

"Now, Mrs. Benson, my daughter swears that your daughter took that bracelet. I just want it returned," Mr. Higgley said.

"I don't care what your daughter said. Did she see Mattie take the bracelet? No! Mattie does not steal! And her father and I raised her to tell the truth," Mrs. Benson countered.

"But she saw Angel put it in her desk," insisted Mrs. Higgley.

"No, Angel says she saw her. Mattie told me she wasn't paying any attention to your daughter," replied Mrs. Benson. "Listen, I took off from work today to come here but I'm not going to put up with this kind of talk. Who do you think you are to accuse my daughter?"

"Please." Mr. Ashby tried to calm the angry parents. "I'm not saying that Mattie took the bracelet, Mrs. Benson, but she does sit next to Angel and she was in the room when Angel put the bracelet in her desk. Also there's been trouble between the two girls." His nose twitched.

"Yes, trouble that Angel has caused," Mama said. "What you're implying, Mr. Ashby, is that Mattie stole that bracelet. You are wrong."

"Look, I want this matter settled. I paid a lot of money for that bracelet and I want it back and the child who stole it punished," demanded Mr. Higgley.

Angel started to say something, but her father

hushed her. Mattie sat quietly and watched her mother argue in her defense. When the meeting was over, the principal refused to suspend Mattie until there was some solid evidence, even though Mr. Higgley protested vigorously. After the meeting, Mattie hugged her mother.

"Now, enough of this. I have to get to work. Tell Matt to sweep the front hall, and you start dinner," she said. "I'll be home late. I have a meeting."

"What meeting, Mama?"

"Never you mind. I'll be fine. Now you go on and don't worry about this."

As she did every day, Mattie raced home that Monday to see if there was any word from the newspaper.

"It will be there," she said to herself.

Twice she had dialed the newspaper office but hung up before anyone answered. Her time was running out too quickly.

Another week of baby-sitting and waiting, thought Mattie as she looked at the empty mailbox.

TWELVE

The next day Mr. Ashby chose Gina Johnson to collect the homework and ignored Mattie when she raised her hand to volunteer to pass back the reading tests. She felt like a long overdue storm was building up inside of her.

"It's not fair! Everybody treats me like a thief," fumed Mattie, wiping at an unexpected flood of tears.

"Crying over my bracelet," accused Angel, her gray eyes icy cold. "I hope they put you out of school for good," she said, leaning over and pinching Mattie's arm viciously.

Mattie felt the storm break inside her. She jumped up and pushed Angel to the floor. In the silence that followed, Mattie looked around her. Toni's face was troubled, and Mr. Ashby looked furious. Charlene was smiling slyly. Mattie ran out of the room. Her heart was pounding and she was scared. She'd never done anything like this before. She took the steps two at a time and headed for the exit. Then she stopped. Where was she going? What would she say to Mama? To Matt? She realized that she was running away.

She sat down on the stairs. After a few minutes, she got up and headed back to the room. She stood outside the door until Mr. Ashby noticed her and came out.

"Mattie, what is going on?"

"Mr. Ashby, everybody acts like I'm a thief. I can't prove that I didn't take Angel's bracelet, but I'm tired of her bullying me."

Mr. Ashby listened quietly.

"Nobody ever believes she's wrong. She's mean, Mr. Ashby, mean and a cheater, and I don't care if you don't believe me," said Mattie fiercely. Standing up for herself helped to release some of the tension.

"But you were wrong to knock Angel down." Mr. Ashby handed her his handkerchief. Mattie was surprised. She was afraid to use it.

"Use it, Mattie. That's what handkerchiefs are for — blowing noses."

"She pinched me," Mattie said. "See, you can see it." A bruised area stood out against her skin.

"I want to get this mess between you two resolved as much as you do, Mattie. It has dragged on for too long. This is no good for the morale of the room, for me, or for you." He spoke quietly.

"Do you believe me?"

"Well, let's say that I'm not as sure as I was," he admitted.

"Thanks, Mr. Ashby. Thanks a lot," Mattie said, blowing her nose and handing back the handkerchief.

"Your coming back was the right thing to do, Mattie. Now, go wash your face."

When Mattie took her seat later, she was surprised to see that Mr. Ashby had moved Angel to a seat across the room. Mattie stared at Charlene, whose nervous jerks reminded Mattie of a scared rabbit. *She's the one*, Mattie thought. *Toni is right.*

During recess, Mattie stood alone on the playground, watching Angel, Charlene, and Toni. What was she doing here all alone? What was she waiting for? As she strode over to the group, Toni came toward her and tried to motion her away.

"Toni, I can't keep waiting for something to happen. I have to face it and make it happen," Mattie insisted.

"Mattie, wait. I know what I'm doing. Please," begged Toni.

Mattie shrugged Toni off and faced her accuser. "Angel, I did not steal your precious bracelet. Mr. Ashby believes me. Go ask him!" said Mattie.

Angel's eyes widened.

"What are you talking about? You liar! He knows you stole it!" she yelled.

"You're wrong. Maybe somebody stole your bracelet or maybe you're just pretending," Mattie challenged.

Angel looked from Toni's set face to Mattie's determined one. She started to turn away.

"Running away, huh, Angel? Because you know I'm telling the truth?" Mattie demanded.

"I'm not running away, Mattie. I know *you* stole my bracelet. Didn't she, Charlene? You saw her do it. You told me you did."

"Sure, sure I did. I saw her take it, Angel." Charlene cowered, aware of the crowd gathering around them.

"No. You couldn't have seen Mattie steal the bracelet, Charlene." Toni spoke so quietly that only the inner group of curious onlookers heard her.

"What are you talking about?" said Charlene.

Angel looked from one face to the other.

"Explain this," said Toni, taking the gold and pearl bracelet out of her coat pocket. "I tried to tell you, Mattie, but I didn't have a chance." She handed the shining bracelet to Mattie.

"Where did you get my bracelet?" demanded Angel, trying to grab it away. "Stole it yourself, huh, Toni? I knew you were just playing up to us. Right, Charlene?"

"Right, Angel," Charlene said, shrinking back and

shoving her hands into her jacket pockets. She tried to push through the crowd, but Mr. Ashby stood directly in her way.

"What's going on here?" asked the teacher.

"Toni found Angel's bracelet," said Mattie, holding it out to the teacher.

"Toni took my bracelet and she's trying to blame it on Charlene," Angel was shouting.

"Be quiet, Angel. Toni, what have you got to do with this business?"

"Charlene and I walked to school together this morning. She kept putting her hand into her jacket pocket as if she had something in there. I was suspicious, and I decided to see what it was. I checked her pocket before recess and found the bracelet," said Toni proudly.

"Charlene?" asked Mr. Ashby.

"I didn't take that bracelet."

"Then how did it get in your pocket?" he asked.

"Charlene wouldn't take anything from me. I'm her best friend," pleaded Angel.

"Charlene, did you take the bracelet?" he asked.

"I didn't *steal* it," Charlene whined.

"Charlene, you didn't, did you?" said Angel. "We're friends."

"Charlene, I want an answer," demanded the teacher.

"I just borrowed it. That's all. I didn't steal anything," Charlene cried.

"You borrowed it? You took it!" Angel shouted.

"Yes, I did! So what? You have lots of pretty things. I'm tired of being the ugly one," screamed Charlene.

"I thought we were friends," said Angel.

Toni laughed. "You're too mean to be a friend."

"You shut up," Angel shouted.

"Now, calm down. I want you four in Mr. Richards' office right now."

They all walked across the playground: Charlene twisting in Mr. Ashby's firm grasp; Angel alone; Mattie and Toni, heads together, talking quietly.

"We did it, Mattie. I wonder what's going to happen to Charlene, though? Am I ever glad I waited for her and walked to school with her today. She kept fingering something in her pocket. I don't think she realized what she was doing. I had no chance to get you alone to tell you."

"You are so smart, Toni. You really got them," Mattie grinned.

"It's sad in a way. I don't know why Charlene let Angel treat her so badly."

"Well, maybe they both learned a lesson," answered Mattie. "But you really got me out of a mess."

"That's what friends are for, Mattie."

Mattie felt sorry for Charlene as she watched her clean out her desk before lunch. She had been given two weeks suspension and a severe reprimand from Mr. Richards. Charlene's older brother was waiting by the door to take her home.

Angel put her head down on her desk and stayed like that for the rest of the day. Mattie watched her line up at the end of the school day and walk out alone.

When Mattie got home, she told Matt all about Charlene. And when Mama came home later, Mattie met her at the door.

"Mama, you don't have to go to school anymore. Charlene stole the bracelet and Angel had to apologize to me," said Mattie.

"Mattie, that's wonderful. I wish I could tell that Mr. Higgley off. How did it happen?"

Mattie told Mama and Matt the whole story as the three of them sat around the kitchen table after dinner eating ice cream. It was like old times — almost.

THIRTEEN

By Friday, Mattie jangled like a live wire. Mother's Day was only a week away. If she had won the contest, she reasoned, surely the newspaper would have let her know by now. So, she wouldn't have the money to buy the pin.

Maybe, if the store would give her more time, though, she could give the pin to Mama for her birthday in June. It was worth a try, and if Toni went with her . . .

Mattie's mind wasn't on her schoolwork and, when the bell rang for lunch period, she fairly pounced on Toni.

"Can you go to Stern's with me after school?" she asked. "I want to ask them to give me more time to come up with the money for the pin. I don't think I won the contest or I'd know by now."

"I can't go with you, Mattie, I have to go home. But I'll keep my fingers crossed for you."

The revolving doors of Stern's wrapped around Mattie and pushed her into the busy store. She looked for Mrs. Grover, but the young salesgirl from the previous week was alone at the jewelry counter.

"Can I help you?" she asked, recognizing Mattie.

"Uh, is Mrs. Grover here?"

"No, sorry. It's her day off."

Mattie was sure this young salesgirl wouldn't know as much as Mrs. Grover, but she had no choice. She had to ask.

"Well, here's the receipt for the pin," Mattie began. "I can't pay the balance now. Can you, please, give me more time?"

"I'm sorry. It's against store policy. They'll only hold the pin for you for thirty days. I'm really sorry."

Mattie could see that the salesgirl was trying to help her.

"Well, then, I have to get my money back." Mattie handed over the receipt and waited while the girl hunted through the box of pink slips.

"That's strange. There's a note here that says the

pin was purchased yesterday." The girl looked truly puzzled.

"You mean someone else bought my pin? But that's not fair! How did you know I wouldn't have the rest of the money in time?"

The salesgirl was counting off the days on a small calendar taped on the wall by the cash register. "Your thirty days were up yesterday," she said.

"But I counted the days!" Mattie insisted.

"Did you count the day you put down the deposit?" she asked.

No! The salesgirl was right. Mattie had miscounted by one stupid day. Mattie silently accepted the deposit money and signed the bottom of the pink form. She didn't see the flowers or smell the perfume this time.

"Whoever had enough money to buy my pin, sure was lucky," Mattie mumbled. She jammed the money into her coin purse and wiped at the tears running down her cheeks. She felt miserable.

It was late when she got home and Matt had already come in and started dinner. He was standing by the stove stirring a pot of chili when Mattie joined him in the kitchen. She told him what had happened as she set the table.

"I told you to spend your money on something that made sense," he reminded her. "I know you feel bad, but Mama likes a lot of things. You can buy her something else."

"I don't want to buy her anything else," Mattie argued. "I want her to have that pin whether you think it's right or not."

"Hey, I'm sorry. But don't get mad at me."

Mattie slumped down on her chair and spooned chili on a slice of wheat bread. "Where's Mama?" she asked.

"I don't know. There was no note. I'm kind of worried," Matt confessed.

"Maybe she just forgot to leave a note."

"I don't think so — I wish I knew what was going on with her."

Before the twins got much further discussing Mama's problems, they heard her key turn in the front door lock and went out into the hall.

"Mama, where were you? We've been worried about you," said Matt.

"Just taking care of something. Did Mrs. Rausch call?" Mama asked.

"No. Nobody called, Mama. Did you eat? Matt made chili. How about chili and salad?" Mattie asked.

"Sounds good." Mrs. Benson hung up her coat and followed the twins into the kitchen.

Matt fixed a bowl of chili for his mother and put it down in front of her.

"Mmmm. Did you add something, Matt?" she asked when she tasted the chili.

"Yeah, a few spices. Eat some more," he said proudly.

With Matt and Mama beaming, Mattie's sad face looked out of place in the circle.

"Mattie, what's wrong? I thought you'd be happy now that that bracelet business was settled," her mother said.

"Oh, I am. It's just that we've been worried about you. You work so hard and get home so late — "

"Well, I think it's time I explained where I've been going," Mama said. "I'm seeing a therapist. Her name is Mrs. Potter. She's a psychologist."

"What's a psychologist, a therapist?" Matt asked.

"A person who's gone to school and been trained to help people with their personal problems. Mrs. Potter is a good woman and she's helping me deal with your Daddy's death — and being responsible for raising you two alone."

"You mean you go and talk to her and she talks to you," Mattie said.

"Yes, that's what I mean. How did you know?"

"Because of Mrs. Stamps. When I go and talk to her, she helps me," Mattie explained.

"Well, Mrs. Potter helps me to help myself. Remember when we went to the show?"

The twins looked at one another and nodded.

"She told me that I had to take small steps to pull us together as a family. Going to the show was one of those steps."

"We did have a good time, Mama," said Matt. "Like when Daddy was alive."

"Yeah." His mother nodded. "Mrs. Potter and I talk about your father a lot — and about you two — and about my work. I have some good news about that. Mrs. Potter told me I didn't have to be afraid of Mrs. Rausch. I do a good job of taking care of this building and I should tell her so."

"*Right on*, Mama," Matt said.

"Well, I told Mrs. Rausch that I needed some security for my family and I asked her for a two-year contract. I got it, too."

"Mama, that's wonderful," the twins shouted.

"How often will you go see the therapist?" Matt asked.

"I'm going to see her until I get better adjusted to your father's death and being a single parent. That's what we agreed."

"When Mrs. Stamps and I talk, I end up feeling better," Mattie said.

"I guess I work out my problems when I paint," Matt said, thoughtfully.

"This is no miracle, believe me, kids. It's hard work and I come home plenty of nights scared and worried. But I believe we can make it. I'm glad I told you," she said. "Now let's get this kitchen cleaned up and go look at some television. Say, was there any mail today?"

"Oh, I forgot," Matt said. "I left it in the living room. There was a letter for you, Mattie."

"For me!" Mattie was almost afraid to go look.

FOURTEEN

Mattie turned the envelope over in her hands. What did it say? She shook her head when her mother asked if she wanted to open it in private. Mattie pried it open. She skimmed the first few lines. Then she put it down.

"Good news or bad news, Mattie?" asked her mother.

"Don't worry, twin," comforted Matt.

Once more she lifted the single sheet of paper and this time she read it out loud.

Dear Miss Benson,

We are pleased to inform you that you have tied for first place in our Third Annual Mother's Day Essay Contest. Our editors read dozens of letters before they selected the winning entries.

We hope you can be present with your mother

at our office to receive your prize and have your photograph taken. Friends and close family are welcome.

A representative from our office will be contacting you to confirm the date and time. Congratulations!

Henry Phillips
Editor-In-Chief
South Side Daily

"Mattie, you won!" Matt shouted.

"What is this all about?" asked Mrs. Benson.

"I won the contest, Mama. I did it! Me, Mattie Mae Benson." Mattie waved the letter in the air, like a banner.

"What contest?" asked her mother, reaching for the letter.

"The essay contest in the *South Side Daily* about what your mother means to you. First prize is fifty dollars and we go to a fancy place for dinner. Toni told me about it, and I've been waiting to hear from them." The words came out in a rush.

"You wrote about what your mother means to you, Mattie?" asked her mother. "And you won!"

"Yes, Mama."

"What's this about a tie?" Matt asked. "Does that mean you have to share the money?" He was reading the letter over his mother's shoulder.

"I don't know. It's too late anyway," said Mattie.

"Too late for what?" inquired her mother.

"Something I wanted to give you," said Mattie. "But I can't do it now."

Mrs. Benson looked confused, but she didn't push for more answers.

"My daughter has won a contest in the *South Side Daily* for writing an essay about me. Mattie, you did that for me?" Mrs. Benson's eyes suddenly brimmed with tears.

"Can we go?" Mattie asked.

"Honey, of course. I'll wear my best dress and Matt will wear his new blue suit." Her mother laughed happily.

"Great! Mama. I want Toni to be there, too. She deserves to be. She helped make it happen. Is that okay?"

"If that's what you want, Mattie."

That night Mattie slept with the letter and her father's photograph under her pillow. She wondered what she should tell Toni.

On the Saturday before Mother's Day, Mama selected a floral print dress from her closet. Holding it up in one hand, she smiled at Mattie.

"Your father and I used to go dancing every month. This was his favorite dress. He said I looked like Lena Horne when I sashayed by him wearing this. I've lost enough weight to wear it again," she said.

"Mama, should I wear my skirt and blouse from Stern's?"

"Oh, no, that's good enough for school, but not for this occasion."

Mattie tugged nervously at her pajamas. What else did she have to wear?

"Look in your closet. You'll find something," urged her mother.

"But, Mama, that's all I have. Everything else is too short or too old," said Mattie, going to her room.

"You just can't tell. I'm going to get Matt started."

Mattie looked through the clothes in her closet. Old shirts, old dresses, and worn-out blouses lined the rack. Then she saw it. A brand-new yellow dress with a stand-up ruffled collar.

"Mama, it's beautiful," said Mattie, holding the dress against her as her mother walked in.

"I decided that Mother's Day was going to be Family Day for us. So I got everybody a present," said Mama. "I can hear that Matt found his."

"Mama, where did these paints come from? And the paper?" Matt said, rushing into Mattie's room.

"From me, for all your help these past six months." She hugged them both.

Toni arrived on time, puzzled and curious. Mattie had just told her that she had a surprise, and she should come over on Saturday for a party.

"What's the surprise? Come on," said Toni.

"Now, Toni, be patient. We *are* going to a party," said Mattie.

Mama decided that they would take a taxi. Still, the drive to the newspaper office was too slow. Toni was unusually quiet. When she looked at anyone, it was Mattie, and then only briefly.

When they arrived at the large brick building that housed the *South Side Daily*, Matt walked in first and held the door open. Mattie had to push Toni through the front entrance.

An office to the right read, PHILLIPS, EDITOR-IN-CHIEF. Matt opened the door. A tall black man greeted them.

"You must be the Bensons. Good. And who is Mattie?" Mama introduced Mattie and the man took his glasses off and held out his hand.

"Young lady, that was some essay you wrote. Seldom in my years as an editor have I been so touched."

Toni stared down at the floor.

"And you must be Toni?" he said, holding out his hand.

"Yes," Toni looked at Mattie. "But how do you know my name?"

"You'll see," he promised. "And you're Matt."

"Yes, sir."

"And you're the mother Mattie wrote about, Mrs.

129

Benson." He extended his hand once more and then invited them all to sit down. Mr. Phillips seemed to be enjoying the confusion.

"Mr. Phillips, what did I win?" asked Mattie, sitting forward on the edge of her chair.

"In time, in time. Let's talk while the photographer sets up. Do you mind our running your essay in tomorrow's edition?" He twirled a pencil in his fingers.

"No, that's all right," said Mattie slowly.

Toni stole a look at Mattie.

"What would you like to win?" he asked.

Mattie didn't know what to say.

"You ready for some pictures, Mrs. Benson? Mattie?" he inquired.

They nodded.

"Good. Let's get some shots, before and after." He ordered in crisp tones. "Ready, Davis?"

"Ready, Mr. Phillips. I'd like a couple of group shots and then I'll take them as they come." The young woman handled her equipment expertly and efficiently.

After the photographing session, Mr. Phillips invited everyone to sit down again.

"Mattie, I'd like you to share your essay with us," he said.

Toni took a deep breath.

"All of it?" asked Mattie.

"Well, it isn't very long," he replied.

Mattie got up and took the piece of paper he handed her. She faced her mother, brother, and best friend.

Dear Mr. Phillips,

My name is Mattie Mae Benson. My father is dead. My mother loves my twin brother, Matt, more than me. I love my mother but I have a hard time telling her. I wanted to win this contest so much that I asked my best friend, Toni, to write an essay. I thought I had a better chance to win with her essay. I'm so bad with words. If I could only sing and tell you how I feel about my mother, I could win. I want to win the money so I can buy my mother a beautiful pearl and gold pin at Stern's. It is beautiful and special, just like my mother. This is my essay. I'm sending it to you because I love my mother in good times and bad times. But I love her too much to try to win with a lie.

Sincerely and truthfully,
Mattie Mae Benson

The room was quiet. Mattie looked at her mother.

"But, Mattie, I do love you," said Mrs. Benson with tears in her eyes.

"I just wanted you to know how sad I feel when you cry and miss Daddy and call for Matt and not me," said Mattie.

"But I love you, Mattie. Maybe I don't understand

you the way I do Matt, but I love you," she repeated.

"I want to be yours, too, Mama," said Mattie.

Her mother got up and hugged Mattie while the camera clicked away.

"You are mine — my only girl," said her mother.

Mr. Phillips cleared his throat. "I think it's time to find out what this very unusual essay has won for you, Mrs. Benson," he said.

Matt and Toni leaned forward as Mr. Phillips reached behind his desk and lifted a large, gaily wrapped box. He handed it to Mattie's mother.

Mrs. Benson touched the bow as if it were made of fragile crystal. Taking her time, she peeled off the paper. Finally, she lifted the cover of the box and laughed as she took out another box. It was wrapped in gold foil. Mattie expelled her breath as Mama unwrapped it. This time, she held a small blue box in her hand. She looked at Mattie as the camera whizzed away.

"It's the most beautiful thing I've ever seen in my life. Mattie, look!" Mama said.

In wonderment, Mama held out the lovely gold pin with the single moon of pearl.

"But how?" Mattie searched Mr. Phillips' face for an explanation.

"Got it, Davis?" hollered the editor.

"Yes, sir!" the photographer answered.

"Mr. Phillips, it's my pin! The one they said somebody had bought!"

"Yes, it is," he replied.

"But how?" asked Matt and Toni.

"Mattie, the editorial board felt that you deserved more than a check for fifty dollars and a dinner. Your essay was worth the pin you dreamed of," he said.

"You mean you bought it?" she asked.

"Only after we explained what this was all about," he grinned.

Mattie grinned and hugged Toni.

"I wanted to tell you about the essay, but you wouldn't let me," said Mattie.

"I know. I just didn't want to think about it again," said Toni.

Mattie looked at each person in the office. After thanking Mr. Phillips nine more times, Mattie reached into her purse and took out Toni's essay.

Mrs. Benson watched her daughter proudly.

"Toni, thanks for being so willing to help me. I know that you didn't want to do it. And now I know I shouldn't have asked you. It wasn't fair to you. This is a good essay but I had to find my own words — win or lose," Mattie said.

For once, Toni was at a loss for words. She just nodded and accepted her essay.

After obtaining a few more facts and pictures, Mr. Phillips wished Mrs. Benson a happy Mother's Day and showed them out.

"Just a minute, Mama." Mattie ran back, knocked

on Mr. Phillips' door, and peeked in.

"Yes, Mattie?" he said, looking up from the papers on his cluttered desk. "Anything else the *South Side Daily* can do for you?"

"No, sir, I just wanted to give you this." She ran over and kissed him on the cheek.

"You earned that pin, Mattie, and the paper is proud to acknowledge your efforts," he said.

The next morning, Mattie stood next to Toni in the choir. Mrs. Stamps, gaily dressed as always, was seated in back of Mama, who was in the front pew wearing the pin on her floral print. Matt sat beside her, looking proud and happy in his blue suit. Mama had also loved his present. It was a portrait of the three of them, and he'd framed it himself. Mama had hung it in the living room, covering one of those sad, empty spaces.

Mattie looked out at them. *I have made a place for myself in the circle of my family*, she thought. *It's still a bumpy circle and maybe Matt will always be Mama's favorite, but that's okay. At least I have a place with Mama.*

Mattie walked to the microphone to sing a solo. Tapping her feet in time to the organ and the tambourines, she let her voice fly out and soar. Mattie felt a wonderful, tingling sensation all over her body, as if her skin was stretching and falling away, leaving her free to grow some more.

ABOUT THE AUTHOR

Candy Dawson Boyd has based the *Circle of Gold* on her own experiences as a young girl growing up in Chicago. When she was 12, Candy entered a writing contest sponsored by the local newspaper. "My mother worked very hard to keep our family together," she says, "and winning that contest was my way of saying 'Thank you, Mama.'"

Ms. Boyd lives in northern California, where she is a Professor in the School of Education at Saint Mary's College of California.